The Man in the Cellar

Palle Rosenkrantz

Originally Published as *Amy's Kat* in 1907

Kazabo Publishing

Translation and Foreword © 2018 Kazabo Publishing

Garamond 12/16/22
ISBN: 978-1-948104-13-5
P011

Cover image courtesy of Bob Borson FAIA

Kazabo books are available at special discounts when purchased in bulk or by book clubs. Special editions of many of our books can also be created for promotional and educational use. Please visit us at kazabo.com for more information.

Table of Contents

Foreword

With our rich English mystery novel tradition, we can easily forget that other countries have their own thriving mystery genres. We have all heard of Sherlock Holmes but how many of us have heard of Dagobert Trostler, who is widely known in the German-speaking world as the Sherlock Holmes of Vienna? Agatha Christie is a household name in both the UK and the U.S., but Sven Elvestad is equally famous in Scandinavia.

Baron Palle Adam Vilhelm Rosenkrantz, born in 1867, is the father of the Danish mystery novel. In the early part of the 20th century, he was one of the best-selling authors in Scandinavia and Germany. To this day, the Palle Rosenkrantz Prize is awarded annually to the best crime novel published in Danish.

Baron Rosenkrantz, while a member of the aristocracy, was also a pointed social critic and his novels reflect that.

> *The first night Holger Nielsen spent in the new house, he could not sleep. Not because he was not tired, because he was always tired in London. The long walks through the streets, standing in the midst of the cosmopolitan city and following the flow of the people about whom everything individual disappeared, watching the richly dressed, well-groomed crowd that floated past the bright shop windows—always shopping, busily increasing their abundance, and the infinite maze of byroads and lanes in which dirt and poverty lived, where the miserable children of the poor surrounded him while playing, and where the contrast to the abundance of the great streets taught him the elements of socialism—all these walks tired him very much.*

Nowadays, we think of Denmark as a society dedicated to fairness, where corruption is non-existent. But it was not always so. Trained as a lawyer, Rosenkrantz was keenly aware of the bias and outright injustice faced by ordinary people dealing with officialdom and the judicial system. Of course, some of Rosenkrantz's concerns will seem dated to us. But even his quaintest concerns — especially his quaintest concerns — provide a fascinating look at a different world. Scandinavia has not always been IKEA and Legos.

Rosenkrantz was a thoughtful observer not just of society but of human nature and much of what he writes rings as true today as it did a hundred years ago. Many of his novels deal with an unusual moral ambiguity. In a typical mystery, it's easy to tell the good guys from the bad guys, especially by the end of the book. But Baron Rosenkrantz's novels often depart from this comfortable certainty. As in all mysteries, a crime has been committed and must be unraveled. But in that unraveling, it often becomes less and less clear who is the victim and who is the perpetrator. Will invoking the authorities and the power of the state truly bring justice or would doing so be an even greater crime? Agatha Christie's *Murder on the Orient Express* comes close to the flavor of these stories except that, in Rosenkrantz's novels, the central moral dilemma is seldom resolved so easily.

The Man in the Cellar contains a surprising amount of moral philosophy even for one of Rosenkrantz's books. Throughout their investigation, the main characters struggle with the social implications of their actions. Is the correct thing always the right thing? Can there be one rule for society yet another for an individual? Is true objectivity ever possible and how must one act when it is not? Even the question of prejudice rears its head.

Perhaps one of the most interesting questions — and one which is very relevant for us today — is to what extent the good of society is predicated on those willing to break the very rules that are necessary for society to exist. Do we maintain our own moral consciences because others are willing to violate theirs? Rosenkrantz turns murder into a sort of moral McGuffin.

You might think that all this thoughtful exploration would make *The Man in the Cellar* tedious and preachy. It does not. The story is engaging and well-plotted, and Rosenkrantz manages to treat the moral questions with a pleasingly light touch. On the question of prejudice, one of the characters teases the other for being unable to shake the idea that the beautiful must also be innocent while in turn, the same character, half-mockingly, assumes that the ugly must be guilty. Rosenkrantz has a pleasantly dry, deft and occasionally self-deprecating sense of humor, even making use of what would now be known as meta-fictional devices to let the reader in on the joke.

Rosenkrantz was an enormously influential literary figure. During his lifetime, he wrote eighty novels and several screen plays. While he remains well-known in Scandinavia and Germany, he is largely unknown in the English-speaking world. We hope you will agree that this is a shame and that it is long past time that this unique voice and his excellent stories were made available to a wider audience.

Chiara Giacobbe

Part 1
Cranbourne Grove 48

Chapter One

"It is dirt cheap, sir, dirt cheap! Three and a half guineas per week for the whole fully furnished house, consisting of studio, two living rooms, a large dining room and three bedrooms—not counting the garden. Electric light in the whole house and gas in the kitchen. It is dirt cheap. And it is only by chance that I can give you the house so cheap."

Mr. Sydney Armstrong clicked his tongue and tapped a walking stick on his brown leather leggings. He was dressed sportily as usual, for sport was his main occupation. In addition, he worked to earn his living as an agent for home sales and rentals. His business was still young, and the staff consisted only of himself and an office clerk.

At the moment he was standing in the corridor of a small house in London's Cranbourne Grove; 48 was the number. The house, a real country house, stood a little secluded within a walled garden in South Kensington, near the museum, the bus, and the subway station.

As always, Mr. Armstrong applied his old business trick: he pretended not to care at all about renting the house, while in reality he was very much interested; there were five pounds to earn, and five pounds would be a tidy sum for a young house agent.

For this reason, too, Mr. Armstrong emphatically brushed his mustache while trying to impart a look as indifferent as possible.

And the bird he wanted to catch had actually started flapping into the net. It was dirt cheap for such a house! Three and a half guineas per week!

The bird, who was a Dane, converted the sum into Danish money. "Three and a half guineas are more than three and a half pounds," he said to himself, because a guinea, according to an ancient tradition— God knows why—is as much as a pound and a shilling. Three and a half guineas are thus three pounds, thirteen shillings, and sixpence, that is, sixty-five Danish kroner.

That was more expensive though than Holger Nielsen had intended. But there was also a studio in the apartment, and in general it was a lovely little house. In addition, Holger Nielsen was not planning to live in it alone, for he had arranged with a doctor Jens Koldby to rent an apartment in London together—and not a floor in one of those enormous apartments, but a real clean, old English cottage with a garden. And Madame Sivertsen, who spent fourteen years as an attendant on an Atlantic steamer and spoke perfect English, would be in charge of their household during the three months they intended to spend in London.

Doctor Koldby was a painter, and therefore the studio was needed.

Holger Nielsen also stroked his small, light-brown mustache and made an effort to negotiate prices.

"Let's say three pounds ten shillings," he suggested.

"We always count with guineas in London," replied Mr. Armstrong. "It's really dirt cheap! You can believe me! The house is not my own; it belongs to an officer who went to Burma. And I have my specific orders. Actually, it should be four guineas. I can go down to three and a half, but not half a penny less."

And Mr. Armstrong tried to look superior but failed because of his thin yellow mustache.

"It's really too much," said Holger Nielsen.

Mr. Armstrong shrugged. "Then let us go," he said. He didn't want to give in, because at three and a half guineas he would get five pounds. And so, he stuck to his demand.

Holger Nielsen, who liked the house, hesitated. And Mr. Armstrong grew hopeful again.

"Show me the house again," Nielsen said finally. And they went in again.

The entrance was small and narrow; it turned into a corridor about twelve feet long and four feet wide, from which a staircase led upwards. Behind it, the corridor narrowed and led to the kitchen and the basement. On either side of the corridor was a door to the two living rooms, each with a window as high as the wall. Toward the back, a door led from the corridor to the small garden with its two elongated grass lawns and a few fig and laurel trees. The two rooms on the ground floor were large, richly carpeted and decorated with old-fashioned and carved furniture. From the room on the right a door led to a corridor running to the rear, at the end of which lay the very spacious and high-ceilinged dining room; it was rather a hall, but quite dark, as it received light only through a window in the ceiling. The old oak furniture was heavy and dark, and the floor was covered with new

3

linoleum, which Mr. Armstrong seemed to fancy.

"It's pretty dark here," said Nielsen.

"Oh, it's always dark on the ground floor of a London house," the agent told him. "It's much lighter up there."

The upper rooms were indeed bright and friendly. The windows of the two bedrooms, which were next to the stairs, looked out onto the sunny side of the garden, and the sun was kind enough today to support Mr. Armstrong. It shone in through the cute little windows with all its might, and the studio with its large skylight was literally flooded with light.

This sunshine put an end to Nielsen's hesitation; it gave a considerable advantage to Mr. Armstrong, for the sun is a rarity in London, especially in South Kensington, which is so close to the Thames with its mists.

"Shall I sign the contract right now?" Nielsen asked.

A sigh of relief sounded in place of the yes. The bird in the net had stopped fluttering.

Holger Nielsen signed the contract and paid half a crown for the stamp. Nothing else. "The owner has to pay all the rest," said Armstrong eagerly; now that he had won the game, he let himself be brought to some amiability.

"Who is the owner?" Asked Nielsen, who wanted to know in whose house he would be living.

"Major Johnson," replied Armstrong. "He went to Burma. Just left. It's a real coincidence that you got the lovely house. The major has just lived in it for a week. Yes, just think. He had bought the house from a friend who had inherited it from his mother. I don't remember his name, I have a poor memory for names, but this mister . . . So-and-so had just sold the house to Major Johnson when, on the following day, he was ordered to go down to the colonies. And there was nothing to do, he had to go. He had wanted to get married, but his bride broke off the relationship and he left without her. Yes, this can happen in countries that have colonies. Be glad that Denmark has none except Spitsbergen. But that's what happened to the major. His friends assure me, he almost leapt with joy to avoid an evil mother-in-law."

You see, Mr. Armstrong—happily contemplating the prospect of five pounds—had begun to joke.

"How about the furniture?" Nielsen asked.

"Oh, the major bought the furniture along with the house. As far as I know, Mr. So-and-so, who inherited it, or his sister, lived here until a week ago. Then he sold it to the major and went his own way."

"And what happened to him?"

"I don't know. I don't know him at all. All I know is that he was unmarried."

Nielsen looked at him, scrutinizing.

"The furniture suggests, however, that a lady has been here. Don't you agree?"

"Yes," said Armstrong, "it must have been his sister who lived here with her husband. He had the studio set up by the way, because he painted, I believe. But, as I said, I don't know anything about the family. I know only Major Johnson; he belongs to the Johnsons of Yorkshire. But you understand nothing about that as a stranger to these parts."

In fact, Nielsen didn't know the Johnsons of Yorkshire and quietly accompanied Mr. Armstrong to his bureau where a proper contract was drawn up and signed. On May 1, Doctor Koldby and Madame Sivertsen were to arrive, and both expected to find everything in order. Now that it was already April 29th, it was time to come to a decision, and Nielsen was overall satisfied with the deal.

Chapter Two

Holger Nielsen was, as we already heard, a Dane. He had studied law, was the son of a government official, thirty-two, and had considerable knowledge. He had originally been in a ministry position but had to retire because a certain stiffness in his back prevented him from crawling in front of his superiors. Then he had tried being a lawyer, but also found that job not suitable because his back had been too stiff for the clients. Then he had thrown himself into the study of crime and shocked all of his conservative relatives with his radical ideas. He was an only son; his parents, both of whom were already dead, had left him a considerable fortune. He now lived on his inheritance and devoted himself entirely to his field of interest—criminology. And this interest had finally led him to London, in whose narrow streets he intended to conduct criminal studies. He had received praise for his great published volume, *Crime*; however, as a strong and healthy man, he despised sitting in his chair and gathering his knowledge from books alone. In fact, he avoided books altogether; using only the material that life itself offered for his study. Of course, it was not his way to roam the so-called criminal quarters and spy on the questionable rabble—he had not come to London to carry out the traditional journey to Whitechapel with two or three copper coins in his pocket. No, what he wanted was to observe the population of a big city in their narrow streets and get to know the conditions of their daily lives; that was to be the starting point from which he hoped to explain abnormal phenomena.

He wanted to understand London, and this visit was just an introduction. First, he must accustom himself to the language and so follow the events on the street and the police station until he could progress to exploring more serious problems.

On May 1, Doctor Koldby and Madame Sivertsen reached London on the train arriving at Harwich at 7:35. They had made their way via Esbjerg staying aboard the steamer until morning to avoid arriving in London by night.

Holger Nielsen had already arranged his belongings to be taken from the wretched boarding house where he had been staying to the new home, and now received the newcomers—with the help of the sun—most cordially.

And he obviously had succeeded.

Madame Sivertsen's chamber lay in the basement near the kitchen; it was a little dark and narrow, but Madame Sivertsen was not difficult to satisfy; she had been used to tight quarters on the steamer, though age had made her quite stout. And now, as she herself had remarked, she had been lazy for a fortnight, she was ready to go to work. And so, she did.

Meanwhile, Doctor Koldby inspected the studio and grunted with satisfaction; it was everything it should be. He immediately unpacked his sketches and paint tubes, set up the easel and adjusted a canvas. He had come to London to make some sketches of the Thames and the docks; he also wanted to study Turner in the National Gallery.

Koldby was a painter of seascapes with the title of Doctor of Medicine; his father—a doctor—had forced him to take this job thirty years ago. Koldby's inclinations, however, went in a different direction, and his father, an old land doctor at Thisted, had scarcely closed his eyes when Koldby threw his stethoscopes and other instruments into the corner and spent the old man's well-earned pennies on paints and canvas. Since he was attracted to the sea, he crossed the ocean to Mexico. From the coast of Florida, where he was shipwrecked, he gradually came, traveling and painting through the country, to New York, later returning home, then traveling to Egypt, where he painted sphinxes and pyramids, and became, as time goes by, an old man of about sixty years. But his back was straight and his spirit young. On a Christmas Eve in Rome, he met Holger Nielsen, and they both took a liking to each other. They became, and remained, friends.

During his many journeys through Egypt, Doctor Koldby had adopted Muslim-like attitudes; he loved the sunrise prayer and abhorred wine. In one respect alone he had not become a good Muslim; the Prophet's teaching about polygamy didn't meet with his approval. He not only detested wine, but also women. And though he had to admit that his hatred of the weaker sex was wholly without reason, since no woman had ever harmed him, he clung to his dislike; he thought that in this way he had been saved from many disappointments.

7

With his colleagues, the professors of fine art, he lived in constant dispute; he declared them all idiots and treated them with disregard, an opinion which they returned in kind.

Otherwise, he was sensible and straightforward.

And now the sun was shining into the studio of the house at Cranbourne Grove 48, warming the back of the painting doctor and conveniently lighting up the sketches he had made of the stormy sea on the journey from Esbjerg.

For Doctor Koldby, it was everything as it should be.

Chapter Three

The first night Holger Nielsen spent in the new house, he could not sleep. Not because he was not tired, because he was always tired in London. The long walks through the streets, standing in the midst of the cosmopolitan city and following the flow of the people about whom everything individual disappeared, watching the richly dressed, well-groomed crowd that floated past the bright shop windows—always shopping, busily increasing their abundance, and the infinite maze of byroads and lanes in which dirt and poverty lived, where the miserable children of the poor surrounded him while playing, and where the contrast to the abundance of the great streets taught him the elements of socialism—all these walks tired him very much.

And yet he could not sleep.

The noise on the street decreased more toward midnight, the wheezing of the motorcars, and the rumbling of the buses became increasingly rare, the coachmen's shouts died away, and the footsteps on the cobblestones began to sound only occasionally. At last everything fell silent, blanketed by the night; only the clock on the nearby tower announced the hours with dull blows.

It was a dark night—no moonlight—and complete silence had finally arrived. And yet Holger Nielsen thought he heard something somewhere in the dark, something he could not decipher, or explain.

It sounded almost like the cry of a child . . . or a cat. Not like a loud cat howling or meowing, but like a very soft, miserable, helpless crying that seemed to come from far away. Nielsen tried not to notice it, tried to find sleep, but the lamentation grew louder and even more miserable. Of course, he knew that there was at least one cat in each house in London, all very well-treated animals that enjoyed some kind of civil rights, under no constraint, and able to pass their lives day and night as they pleased. On the other hand, this cat, if it was a cat, must have been a wretched, maltreated creature mourning in the cellars of the house; because in this house it definitely sat.

After listening for a while, Holger Nielsen rose, put on some clothes, turned on the light, and quietly walked out into the corridor. Again, he

9

could not find out where the sound came from; it sounded vaguely from the depths.

Now Nielsen walked quietly, so as not to disturb his companions, into the kitchen. Once there, he heard a rustling in Madame Sivertsen's chamber and noticed a strip of light under her door.

Madame Sivertsen!" he whispered.

"Is this you, Mr. Nielsen?" her voice asked. "Thank God."

"Aren't you asleep yet?" he asked.

"No," was her answer. "I can't shut my eyes. I always hear something moving."

There was really something moving, Nielsen heard it now as well. The sound was like a soft scratching or creeping and yet again resembled neither of them.

"There must be a cat in the house somewhere, Madame Sivertsen," said Nielsen in a whisper.

"*That* is not a cat," she replied softly, but firmly.

"What else could it be?" he replied. "Listen, now it's howling— Where could the animal be?"

The old woman stepped out of her chamber in an elaborate nightgown with a huge night cap.

"That is not a cat," she repeated, shaking her head causing the ribbons to fly. "There's something in the house, Mr. Nielsen."

Nielsen had to smile, "Do you think the house is haunted?"

She was silent.

"You don't believe in ghosts, Madame Sivertsen?"

The old woman shook her head, "It's definitely not a cat. Something is going on in the house."

"Are you afraid?"

"Me? No. I have a clear conscience—it will leave me alone. But it sounds so frightening."

Nielsen decided to get to the bottom of the matter. He combed the house, stomping on the floor and knocking on the walls. The sound stopped; but as soon as he left the corridor, the lamentation sounded anew.

Finally, the clock struck one.

"Well, now our ghost is going to rest," he said to Madame Sivertsen with a smile. "And I think we must do the same."

Madame Sivertsen shook her nightcap ribbons and jiggled back into

10

her room.

Nielsen also went to bed, finally falling into a restless sleep and dreaming of a huge black cat, who sat purring on the bed in front of him.

He slept very badly that night.

Doctor Koldby, on the other hand, rested in the true sleep of the righteous, and the next morning he had only a mocking laugh for Nielsen and Madame Sivertsen. He was delighted with the house and especially with the studio.

Nielsen spent the whole day searching all the rooms, but without finding a cat or anything else noteworthy. Finally, he put the matter out of his mind and left for a walk.

The very next night both he and Madame Sivertsen were unable to close their eyes again; the cat was heard again.

This time, they woke the doctor, who had to admit that something was making a noise. The doctor also thought it was more of a cat than a ghost, and the two friends decided to do a very thorough investigation the next day.

Such was the decision of their second night, which was to be carried out on the third day.

Chapter Four

"Look, Doctor, there—that's a tiny cellar, isn't it? Nielsen gestured toward a coal cellar with a round iron plate to close the hatch. Can you see anything else in it?"

Nielsen and the doctor were on their expedition. It was bright daytime now and they were determined to find the cat. It had to be in the house . . . it could only be in the basement . . . but the basement, the only one in the house, was empty. The animal was no longer howling and seemed to have retired after the efforts of the previous night.

"We dreamed, my dear friend," said the doctor, "unless Edgar Allan Poe's tale of the cat, walled in with a corpse, is to be realized in this little London cottage. That would be something for you, right, Mr. Criminal Investigator! A cat in the walls calling for justice with its whining and meowing. Then the ghost we heard at night would not be so strange. Well, let's go back to daylight."

They went upstairs and around the outside of the cottage again. The wing that housed the dining room had been rebuilt and had its own roof; it was built like the rest of the house out of brown bricks, while the pedestal was made of cement bricks. To allow for air circulation small gaps had been cut into the pedestal, which were protected by iron bars. Nielsen walked around the outside, poking at the gaps with a stick to see whether they led to a cavity.

Suddenly he paused.

"Doctor," he said, "look, here's a low room only tall enough to give shelter to a cat. Look, there's the cat inside!"

"Wriggle in," replied the doctor sardonically. "Make yourself thin and crawl through the bars. There is no other way."

"Well, the floor of the dining room, which must be here, is covered with linoleum."

"Are you going to rip it open?" cried the doctor in horror.

"Well, now," said Nielsen, "I want to get to the bottom of this, because I want my night's sleep—and otherwise we would be acting cruelly toward the cat."

"How on earth do you think the beast got in there? The bars are barely wide enough to let a mouse through."

"Oh, for example, through a trapdoor, perhaps hidden under the linoleum," replied Nielsen, who was already hurrying toward the corridor door.

The doctor followed him—almost annoyed. As always, he was the more stubborn of the two, though he had to admit that Nielsen's guess could be the right one.

The linoleum was removed, and lo and behold, there was indeed a trapdoor in the floor looking down into a cellar-like room that had no steps leading into it. And no sooner had the light penetrated the small square opening into the cellar than a long, thin, gray cat leaped out, fleeing, half-alive, full of fear, with stiff, awkward movements, through the corridor into the garden, where it vanished.

"That was the cat," said Nielsen.

"That was it," said the doctor, "but how in heaven's name did it get in there?"

"Let's get a lamp and a ladder," said Nielsen. "Then we'll climb down. I mean, there's more to it."

It was a very low cellar to which the air had access only through the narrow, barred gaps. It appeared to have been a wine cellar, but at the moment it was empty. But in one corner stood a big long box with a nailed lid.

Nielsen stepped toward it to take a closer look.

"Watch it, it's going to explode," joked the doctor. "You know what? A Russian terrorist lived here and kept his stock of dynamite in this cellar . . . By the way, it looks like lime has been strewn there. Right, it's lime."

"Wait a minute," said Nielsen, "I'll fetch a crowbar."

The doctor stood with the lamp in his hand and waited, whistling until Nielsen returned with a chisel and crowbar. "You will see, Mr. Criminal Investigator, finally, there's a corpse in the box. Just like in Edgar Allan Poe!"

Nielsen tore at the lid. "Shine the light here, Doctor," he said, a little excited.

The doctor—still whistling—came up with the lamp. Suddenly he fell silent. "It really looks as if . . ." he said, still joking, but suddenly his voice cracked hoarsely—"There under the lime—lies a cloth—Holy

God—there really is a corpse in the box!"

The doctor put the lamp on the floor, and then they set to work. Nielsen brushed off the lime and tore at the remaining lid with a chisel. Neither spoke, but after a few minutes of hard work the body of a man lay on the damp stone floor of the cellar. His face was not visible; it had been destroyed with acid or some other caustic substance. His clothing consisted only of a nightgown with an old scarf around it.

The doctor unwrapped the scarf. "Hold the lamp close—this way," he whispered to Nielsen.

Nielsen did so, and the doctor began his examination.

"There's a small oblong wound in the chest. Murder! The man was murdered, packed in the box and taken down here. And on that occasion the cat must have crept in as well."

Nielsen didn't reply. He knelt, bending over the dead man as the doctor continued his examination; he was a middle-aged man, moderately tall and exceptionally well-built. There were no tags in his clothing, but it was of a fine cloth.

"It's good that Madame Sivertsen is not here," Koldby remarked, "she would surely have fainted."

This remark summoned Nielsen back to daily life. "We should go back upstairs," he said.

But the doctor didn't want to go. "I have to finish my examination first. After all, I am a doctor by profession. Killed with a deadly weapon, wrapped in a lady's scarf, packed in lime, and finally locked in a box to be forgotten . . . if the cat had not intervened! This is woman's work, and it seems to have happened recently . . . wait—How long can a cat live without food?"

"We should go up," repeated Nielsen. "And when Madame Sivertsen comes home, let's keep silent about what we've found."

So, they went up to the dining room, closed the trapdoor, and replaced the linoleum above it.

14

Chapter Five

While the sun shone happily outside, the two men sat silently in one of the lower rooms, thinking. This was a serious matter.

Nielsen spoke first, "I think it's best I go to the police and report the whole story. A murder has recently been committed in this house. As for the dead, I hardly believe that we have to identify him, it is the major; Mr. Armstrong told me that he had lived in the house for only four days. The murderer, it seems likely, is the heir whose name Armstrong had forgotten. What do you think, Doctor?"

Koldby sucked on his pipe.

"I think nothing," he said after a while. "The crime has now reached the point where the doctor has nothing else to say. I recorded the death and made my hypotheses about its cause. Now it's the legal system's turn. Of course, the most common path that every good citizen would follow in such a case is to the police—it is also most convenient! But . . . hmm, yes . . . I confess, it surprises me, that you think first and foremost of the police. And I can only assume that this idea has instinctively appeared to you."

"What do you mean?" Nielsen asked.

"Hmm," replied the doctor through a thick cloud of smoke. "You know that I enjoy your original views on the law, your sympathy toward criminals, and your hatred of everything called policing. But that seems to me to have been all theory. Now that you are facing a real crime for the first time, you talk about the police like anyone else."

Nielsen jumped up, agitated, "But how am I supposed to talk? I can't do anything."

"Well," said the doctor with a smile, "I also think you can't do anything here. But as you know, I love people who don't just talk about principles, but who also act accordingly. And here you are—a thoroughly modern criminologist—a criminal ally to your fingertips, and the first thing you think about is—the police!"

Holger Nielsen shrugged. "Just because you want to condemn what is normal and want everything different, does not mean you are cut off from using existing facilities. My radical ideas and theories are *one* thing, they set me an attainable goal. But the existing circumstances and conditions are another thing; they have to keep the machinery going and just as long as the radical ideas haven't become reality, they must be taken into account and respected accordingly. The true radicalism is one that pursues one's ideas to the last consequences, spreads them among the people, throws down the old ideas, and then waits quietly for the new ideas to win their victory in public opinion. Not revolution, but evolution."

Doctor Koldby nodded and said, "That's right. And I know it all very well. I may even be wrong. But if I were you, I would prefer to work hand in hand with my theory. I mean, you and those like you, who despise the law and the police, have no right to call 'police!' You yourself must come up with your own theory of proof, your principles of responsibility, your conclusions, and so on.

"You find a dead man lying in a box covered with lime in your own cellar. You don't know who he is, because his face is unrecognizable and his clothes give no indication of who he might be. He seems to have been murdered. As for me, I haven't the slightest interest in whether you hand over the body to the police or leave him the basement. The man is dead, and no other housemate could bother me less than a dead man in the cellar. And we got rid of the cat as well.

"But you, my friend, you must have a purely scientific interest in the case. Wouldn't it be interesting for you to see what you can find out? Treat it as a kind of house sport. As far as I know, there is no obligation for us to report this murder to the police. The man is already dead."

"I don't know if there is an obligation in England to report the finding of a corpse," interrupted Nielsen.

The doctor laughed dryly. "There's the lure of the law again! Sir, as far as I'm concerned, do whatever you want. But at least be warned, because we'll get into a hell of a lot of trouble if you file a report; we risk detention, interrogation, and the rest. The man's body is still fresh!"

"Would that be a reason for you to refrain from filing such a report?" Nielsen asked him.

"Frankly, yes! I never pretended to be a social reformer. I wouldn't even raise a finger for you either. I feel very comfortable as I am, and if you were to ask me what I would like to do most, I would reply: let's

16

put our man back in the box, push the box into the corner where we found it, and nail the linoleum over it to get on with our day's work quietly. It is certain that somebody will find the box after us, it isn't our concern; by the first of August we will already have traveled back across the sea."

The doctor leaned back in his chair and kept on smoking; he felt satisfied with his speech, Nielsen could see that.

"We risk being suspected of committing the crime if the body is found later," Nielsen said. "We lived here, found the body, and didn't say anything! It's better, if we face the discomfort right away—now while we have a clear conscience. It would be ridiculous if we displayed even the slightest trace of complicity."

The doctor looked at him sideways. "Your thoughts are becoming even more modern," he said sarcastically. "I remember the last lecture you gave at the Copenhagen Workers Club about guilt and complicity. Yes, those were ideas! You stated that every human act, including crime, should be treated individually. I still remember it very well. The two little radicals, Miss Smith and Miss Smith, were crying! And now, remember, if this corpse is that of a rogue, perhaps, who has wounded his wife or has the ruin of some dozen others on his conscience? Then what? Have you completely forgotten what you said so zestfully about the hounds of justice on the trail of the culprit?"

Nielsen shook his head impatiently up and down, "It is easy for you to talk!" he spluttered.

"And you have an easy job!" the doctor replied dryly. "I've always found your theories to be excellent, but your practice, my dear friend, doesn't differ in the least from that of a justice minister. And so, the whole theory that you invented is limping, it's lame! Yes!"

"We could choose a middle ground," said Nielsen.

"A middle . . . Ha, ha!" laughed the doctor. "Well, just choose your middle ground! It is well known that the middle ground is where everyone stumbles when they are not being whipped for something else."

Nielsen got angry.

"Sometimes you're really foolish, Doctor."

"Oh, very often—most of the time! Always! I confess it openly. But now it is your turn to speak. Get started with your explanation. If it doesn't get too tricky, I hope to be able to follow you, despite my

17

innate stupidity. I'm all ears."

Nielsen paused for a while, leaning against the table.

"Let us suppose," he said slowly, "we do nothing. I don't think we are legally obliged to act. And there are also no moral concerns. The matter is none of our business. We don't know the murdered man, nor do we know by whom he was murdered, or how he was murdered."

"Pardon," said the doctor, "he was stabbed in the chest with a small knife."

"Well, but then we just don't know why! Nor are we citizens of this nation—in this society, we are in a sense free—in short, we haven't the slightest obligation to deal with the matter, if not . . ."

"Unless the law of this country compels us to do so," interrupted the doctor, chuckling.

Nielsen dropped into a chair shouting, "You're impossible today, Doctor. Be satisfied when I tell you that, in my opinion, we are not compelled to report this crime; I will not bother to make any inquiries about what the English law requires for such a case. But—and now you prick up your ears—you have plucked a string in me that vibrates when struck; I do now want to solve this crime. You spoke earlier of the author of the act. Well, the way things are, I hold his fate in my hands."

"Or *her* fate," said the doctor. "The crime looks like a woman's work."

"Fine, *her* fate. If the perpetrator had a right to act, then *she* should keep it, and in order to preserve this right, we must take the matter into our hands."

The doctor interrupted him again. "Into our hands? You mean into yours. I risk being hanged if I meddle. And you, dear friend, let me tell you: you may end up with hell to pay! But perhaps you will then consider yourself a martyr of science."

Nielsen was silent for a moment, then shouted, "Doctor, may it be as it pleases. This is an opportunity to test my theory: I will stand in the place of vengeful justice, I will determine the author of the act, I will judge the criminal on his own terms, and I then will act against him as I would want society to act."

The doctor nodded, "You are a good boy, Nielsen. You look very nice talking like that, and maybe you're right. But you have forgotten one thing. You don't have the same resources that the justice system can draw on."

"I have forgotten nothing," said Nielsen, who now began to gain the upper hand. "My main fight against society is precisely the misuse of violence by the justice system. If I have no such power in my hands . . . well, then I can't abuse it. Doctor, I'll tell you, it works. I take the place of the avenging society, stand before the perpetrator face to face, expose the motives of his act and then decide on the verdict. That's all!"

"I hope you'll enjoy it," the doctor concluded ironically, but there was a glow in his little gray eyes.

"Are you in?" Nielsen asked.

"Okay! I'm already partner in crime anyway. So, I want to remain that way. I will do an extra examination of the dead body for you, as far as I am able without a scalpel. Let us take this opportunity as long as Madame Sivertsen is away, because she must not be told anything."

And they went down to examine the dead man.

Chapter Six

"Look, Nielsen," said the doctor later in the afternoon. "Here are the results of my investigation. I hung up my doctor's lab coat some thirty years ago, but I see that I have remained a real medic, for my report has been so well done that no coroner could do it better."

Nielsen took the paper and read:

"The body was found lying face down in a box on the floor of the cellar. During the examination the body was turned face up. The body was in an extended position, arms were flat by the victim's sides. There is numbness and brown-blue spots, but the decay hasn't yet become perceptible.

"The head was evidently treated after death with a strongly acidic substance, which left traces on the shirt and on the wrapped scarf. This liquid destroyed all the soft parts of the face. The hair on the head was destroyed in strips, but tufts of brownish hair have been left in between.

"The neck shows no signs of strangulation or the like. On the other hand, the chest, just above the left nipple, has a puncture wound about a quarter-of-an-inch long, with jagged edges, evidently caused by a dagger. The wound is deep and seems to enter the heart. According to the bruising under the skin, the bleeding had not stopped when the body was placed in the aforementioned position; the shirt is soaked in blood where it covered the wound.

"Further traces of violence cannot be found. Death must have occurred quickly, if not immediately. How much time has elapsed since then can only be estimated, it may be ten to fourteen days."

"So," cried the doctor with satisfaction, "No professor could have found out more. Maybe the form is not quite correct, but it contains everything that may be worth knowing. And now, after we've examined the body, let's put it back in the box and nail the lid on."

"Good," said Nielsen briefly. He had made his decision.

So they arranged everything as it had been before, and even nailed the linoleum over the trapdoor. They worked calmly and with a clear conscience. They knew what they had decided on, and their decision was firm.

When they were back in the living room after finishing the work and the doctor had re-lit his pipe, he remarked to Nielsen, "Well, you avenger of society, reveal your wisdom. What do you intend to do?"

Nielsen hesitated a bit before answering.

"I must confess," he said, "that my ignorance of the customs of this country makes work difficult . . . I must start with a hypothesis. The corpse itself can't tell us anything else, we agree on that. Everything we know about it is written in your notes. We now have two choices: either we try to establish the identity of the murdered man, and from there we make our inquiries about the perpetrator, or we do the latter directly. The usual way is probably the former, but since nothing more can be found out about the dead man, and what we know is insufficient to establish his identity, I propose to begin by immediately establishing the identity of the murderer. For if we have established the killer's identity, we have the victim as well. That is convenient, isn't it?"

"No doubt," said the doctor.

"We must presume Major Johnson's name as our point of departure. The police would start with it as well."

The doctor interrupted him with a dry laugh, "No, my friend, the police would start with you and with me! In fact, at least we have *the* advantage over the police that we know that *we are* not the perpetrators! But now, continue."

"Major Johnson leads us to Mr. Armstrong. That gentleman is such an unbearable chitchat that we must avoid him whenever we can. Besides, as he said, he himself doesn't know who the heir was."

"Hmm, that sounds suspicious."

Nielsen smiled. "Now *you're* talking like the police! Suspicion everywhere, what? We have no one to suspect, but our job is to build a chain from all existing facts that leads back to its starting point."

The doctor nodded, "We should have kept the cat."

"The cat is up and away," said Nielsen, smiling.

At that moment, the doorbell rang, and Nielsen went out to open it.

It was Madame Sivertsen returning with purchases. She had, as she said, bought supplies for a whole ocean's journey.

"Did you find the cat?" she asked as she stowed her packages.

The doctor shook his head.

21

"Pity!" she said and then strode to the kitchen.

Nielsen and the doctor were just about to resume their topic when they suddenly heard Madame Sivertsen screaming in the kitchen: "Doctor! Mr. Nielsen!!"

They jumped in horror—had they forgotten something?

In the kitchen they found their housekeeper almost breathless; her hand pointed to a corner. And there was a long, thin gray cat.

The doctor looked at Nielsen, and Nielsen looked at the doctor. The cat was evidently devoted to the business of eating; she knew how to help herself.

Around her neck was a small silver chain with a name tag attached to it. Nielsen stepped in, unlocked it, and looked at the tag: there were two words engraved on it, "Amy's Puss."

"That's the cat," said Nielsen. "Now we have two pieces of evidence."

The housekeeper was genuinely indignant with the food thief and wanted to chase her out, but the two gentlemen sided with the animal. "The cat has lived here longer than we have," said Nielsen. "We have to respect Amy's Puss. Now I just want to know who Amy is."

"No doubt the lady who owned the cat," said Madam Sivertsen, somewhat piqued. She was annoyed that the cat was being added to the family and could not understand what the two gentlemen wanted to do with the wretched creature.

Puss, for her part, was not in the least worried about all this; she licked her milk, purred, and pretended to be at home.

And she was actually at home.

Chapter Seven

"But what do you say to this, Minister of Justice?"

With these words, Doctor Koldby entered, a little later that same memorable afternoon, and waved a sheet of paper in the air.

Nielsen looked up, "What do you have there?"

"A love note, my friend, a lovely little card, written by a vigorous lady's hand—of course, without a date, for ladies don't pay much attention to such important details. The content is as follows, 'If everything is supposed to be over between us, then may it be so, but I tell you that you will still regret it!' The signature is 'Amy,' the salutation 'Dear James.'"

Nielsen grabbed the card—yes, there really written was 'Amy'—it was a threatening note from her.

"Now we have four pieces of evidence," said the doctor, "number one the corpse, number two the cat, number three the silver collar, and number four this card! What if the murder was Amy's act of revenge?"

Nielsen nodded thoughtfully, "Armstrong told me that Johnson was glad to have gotten rid of his bride. It is possible that Amy was this bride and—"

"—That Johnson is the body? Hmm, that doesn't seem quite believable to me. The major is undoubtedly a person of prestige and importance who couldn't disappear from the scene so easily and without leaving any trace! Of course, after all, what you suggest is possible: that Amy murdered her lover in revenge, forgetting her cat in the cellar. But it seems very strange to me that the lady should have brought her cat for this purpose, and if she is Johnson's cat on the other hand, then I don't understand why she is called, "Amy's Puss."

"I will admit that you are right," said Nielsen. "We know that this cat belongs to a certain Amy, and we also know that the major quarreled with his lover, named Amy. But we can't guess if these two Amys are one and the same person."

"And that is also not our business," replied the doctor with a smile. "We can only proceed rationally step-by-step. I mean, our problem is, first of all, to find out the full name of the major's mistress, and where he and she are now. And here I mean, Mr. Armstrong, that excellent talker, must be able to tell us something. He certainly knows a lot more than he told you."

"Fine," said Nielsen. "But where did you find this note?"

"In the dining room," was his reply, "it was half hidden behind the wall panel. Yes, there you can see, young man, I'm snooping around and doing all sorts of unlikely things when that's actually *your* department. But now be so good as to visit Mr. Armstrong and pump him for more information on the love affairs of Major Johnson."

The bell outside rang again. Madame Sivertsen went to open the door, and then announced a young lady who wanted to speak to the two gentlemen who had recently moved in.

Nielsen rose hastily.

"See," said the doctor in a low voice, "that's our desired Amy. Isn't there a saying that says the criminal or the perpetrator is pulled by an inexplicable urge back to the scene of the crime? Well, go see her, meanwhile, I'll retire to the corridor and listen."

He did, and Nielsen was left a little excited.

The lady entered. She was young and pretty, of decidedly elegant appearance, dressed in a perfectly fitted, tailor-made dress.

Nielsen bowed.

"My name is Miss Derry," said the lady, "Amelia Derry. Excuse me, please, for disturbing you, but this house was recently occupied by a family friend, who has left now—quite suddenly. It is now probable that letters will arrive for him here. Would you be kind enough to send those letters to an address I'll give you?"

Nielsen bowed. "With pleasure, Miss Derry. May I ask you to give me the name of the gentleman who lived here?"

"Major Johnson—James Johnson of the 17th Lancer Regiment. He went abroad. But he has given this address to many people and it is always embarrassing when letters fall into the wrong hands."

"Be sure," said Nielsen purposefully, "that I will not open your bridegroom's letters."

The lady blushed, "My bridegroom . . . How did you know? . . ."

Nielsen smiled, "Oh, I just put two and two together. But maybe I was wrong. I apologize sincerely."

The lady looked at him sharply. "Major Johnson is not my bridegroom," she said finally, "he's just a relative of mine, and my

24

father promised to send him his letters. Mr. Armstrong forgot to mention this, I assume?"

"Indeed," said Nielsen, "he had indeed forgotten that, although he was otherwise very forthcoming."

The lady looked at him sharply again; she had a way of looking sharply at people she talked to.

At that moment, the door creaked, and, assisted by a gentle nudge from the doctor's boot, the cat slid into the room with a slight mew. The doctor himself remained behind the scenes.

The cat walked across the room and snuggled against the lady's dress.

Nielsen held his breath.

"Is that your cat?" the lady asked.

"No," said Nielsen, "it's Amy's cat."

"Amy's cat?" she asked, and Nielsen heard her voice tremble. It was now his turn to look at her sharply.

"Of course," he replied; "We found the cat here in the house when we moved in recently. She had a collar that I took off; it was silver, and the tag read "Amy's Puss." We thought that the people who lived here before us forgot the cat."

Nielsen spoke very slowly. He was pleased that the lady was sitting in full daylight, so that he could observe her closely, while he himself was more in the shade. In the meantime, the cat had jumped onto the lady's lap. "I would rather it had been a dog," thought Nielsen, "these mouse-catchers flatter anyone with their attentions."

"It's a pretty cat," said the lady, kindly, "but she doesn't belong to the major. As I told you, the major didn't live here. He had bought the house from a friend, a Mr. Throgmorton, and his sister—people he had met in India. The purchase was completed quickly—very quickly."

"Did Mr. Throgmorton live here?"

"I don't think so," she said. "I think nobody has lived here for a long time. The furniture was purchased by the major—But now I've fulfilled the purpose of my visit—and don't want to bother you any longer. Will you promise to pass his letters on to my address?"

"If you'll kindly give me your address . . . or maybe your father's?"

"No, no," she said hastily, "here is my address: Miss A. Derry, Clarendon Road 117, Bayswater."

"And what's to happen to the cat?" Nielsen asked.

25

"She can stay here," she said quickly.

Now the door was opened further and the doctor entered.

"I apologize," he said with exquisite courtesy, "but I am this gentleman's friend—we live together—and since I was working in the next room, I could not help but hear your conversation. It didn't seem like anything private. You spoke of letters to Major Johnson. Please, here is a letter for him. It's already been opened, but not by me, there was no envelope."

The lady turned bright red. She evidently recognized the letter and hastily reached for it.

The doctor looked very serious, "I assure you, Miss, that I haven't opened the letter."

She was obviously aware of revealing herself and tried to regain her composure. "This letter has nothing to do with Major Johnson," she said indifferently, handing it back to the doctor, "and it's none of my business. Someone must have lost it. But now my business here is done. So, I can expect you to send the letters. Please excuse the intrusion, gentlemen—Away, kitty, or I'll step on you! It really seems as if this cat wants to go home with me!"

Miss Derry bowed to the gentlemen with a smile, and Nielsen followed her, hurrying out, through the garden to the outer gate.

When the two friends were together again, they held a council of war.

The lady's name was Amelia—Was she Amy? She acted as if she were a friend of the major—was she his former fiancée? She denied the cat—she denied the letter—Was she the writer? Was she a murderer? Was the body in the cellar Major Johnson?

So, the questions followed each other, one upon the next.

"Would you have arrested this lady, if you had the power?" the doctor asked. "She seems suspicious enough, and she was clearly lying. The letter was probably from her; it is only because of that letter she had come. And the cat seems to belong to her as well. Would you have arrested her?"

"No," said Nielsen.

There was a knock on the door from the postman who delivered an envelope bearing the return address of the estate agent. Nielsen received it; its content was:

I forgot to ask you to send me all the letters that arrive for Major Johnson—to me alone, to no one else. Perhaps a request has already been addressed to you from another party, but I beg you not to obey such a request, but to send the letters only to me; this is most important. I'll take the liberty to visit you at half past eleven tomorrow morning. —Sydney Armstrong.

The doctor turned to Nielsen, "Now, would you have arrested her?"

"No," repeated Nielsen, "but I think Miss Derry has every reason to be pleased that she didn't find a couple of Scotland Yard detectives here instead of us."

The doctor nodded. "That's right, because you are always quick in your suspicions. Although, say, does this lady look as if she could kill the major and put him in a box?"

"Absolutely not!" Nielsen asserted firmly.

The doctor patted him on the shoulder, laughing. "My friend, you're on the wrong track again. Because this girl is pretty, well dressed, and ladylike, you can't be suspicious of her, though she is obviously lying through her teeth. If, on the other hand, it was some stout fellow with squint eyes and other marks of inherited inferiority, you would have bunged him in jail at the first possible opportunity."

Nielsen nodded. It annoyed him, but the doctor was right.

"Well, I think it's time to get this matter out of our heads for today," the doctor finally said. "Tomorrow is another day, and then we will see what this excellent Mr. Armstrong has to tell us. Tonight, I think, let's go to a theater and see how miserably Shakespeare is performed here in England."

Chapter Eight

It was a sharp cross-examination that Mr. Armstrong had to endure the next day when he arrived at the house at half-past eleven. And the news which Nielsen and the doctor drew out of him bit by bit was, in brief, the following:

Major Johnson was a man of nearly forty years, of medium height and well-built, so that he could well be the man in the box. He had not gone to Burma, as that was what Mr. Armstrong had come up with to justify the rental of the house. The truth was that Major Johnson had regretted buying the house after dropping his decision to marry Miss Amy Derry. And he had done the latter because he had fallen in love with Mr. Throgmorton's sister, a Mrs. Weston, who had lived in the house with her husband and her brother for quite some time.

Throgmorton, from whom the major had bought the house, was a friend of his from India; Armstrong didn't know him, he only knew that he was a painter. Weston, who had formerly been in the army, was now an invalid—apparently half-crazy. After all, Mrs. Weston was very beautiful. Armstrong had only met Major Johnson once, and he believed that he was no longer in the army but had run away with Mrs. Weston.

That was all Armstrong knew about the family; he had not told Nielsen earlier because Throgmorton had forbidden him to do so. It was, after all, something of a scandal. And at his behest, the agent had also written yesterday's note requesting any letters that might arrive. Throgmorton himself, he said, now lives in Hjørring, a place in Denmark Armstrong had never previously heard of.

All of this news was gradually absorbed by Nielsen, who played his role as examining magistrate perfectly. Mr. Armstrong tried to avoid the inquiry, but Nielsen knew how to make him stay on topic by invoking Miss Derry. Nielsen called the whole affair a scandal, which, if the Derry family wanted, could ruin Mr. Armstrong's reputation; for he had been involved in the conspiracy that Mr. Throgmorton and his sister had obviously committed, and since Mr. Derry, the father of the abandoned bride, was a respected man, it could be a very dangerous

28

affair for Mr. Armstrong.

Mr. Armstrong was forced to admit all; he was not a very gifted man, only greedy and ashamed when he saw his lies revealed. Nielsen promised to keep his secrets, especially since the whole affair didn't really concern him.

The two partners in justice had traveled far that day.

"Doctor," said Nielsen, when Armstrong left, "I think we'd best turn to the police."

"Ah," cried the doctor, "already tired of the matter?"

"No, but it seems to me we should let the justice system proceed in its official form. I don't doubt that the murdered man is Major Johnson, and I am convinced that this Throgmorton and his sister— and perhaps his brother-in-law—have murdered the major and are now enjoying the fruits of their crime abroad."

The doctor smiled.

"You're a legal scholar, Nielsen, that's the trouble. You are blind to all but the official perspective. Yesterday you thought Miss Derry was guilty, though you wavered for all of two minutes because of her attractive appearance. Today you've been listening to that talkative man named Armstrong and now you think Throgmorton is the culprit, and finally, you want to drop any consideration in favor of Miss Derry, who would be most inconvenienced by this affair, and hand the matter over to the police.

"Aside from Miss Derry, you have also promised your silence to Mr. Armstrong, and if he opened up so much to you, he did so only in the good faith that you would keep your promise. You risk ruining Miss Derry, because remember what it means to turn a girl over to the gossipmongers of the halfpenny press who would then publish her private history in all its pages in large letters. And the alleged killers, the Throgmorton party? They would be the only ones who would benefit from your police report. The news would be telegraphed across Europe at once, and the Throgmortons and Westons, if their hands are not clean, would flee from Hjørring to God-knows-where as quickly as possible.

"By the way, I don't understand why these people moved to Hjørring, of all places. Here, too, we can see a stroke of fate. London and India are outside our reach, while we should be able to do something in Hjørring."

Nielsen said nothing.

"Besides," the doctor went on, "it's not at all certain that the Throgmorton party murdered Johnson—nor even that Johnson was really the murder victim. Remember, also Miss Derry or a member of her family may have killed the major in revenge—don't forget Amy's cat, and the threatening letter. And remember, finally, that it may have been also the major who tried to get Mrs. Weston's husband out of the way. That's also a very reasonable assumption . . ."

"Or that Mrs. Weston's husband killed the major."

"That is also possible. In short, we still know too little. It would be best if you went to Miss Derry's house tonight to find out if she lied to us yesterday. I have already observed that you are excellently suited as an examining magistrate."

Again, it was the doctor who tipped the scales, and Nielsen set off for Clarendon Road 117 that afternoon.

Chapter Nine

Miss Derry didn't live in the house on Clarendon Road 117, only a seamstress lived there, whose customer she was. Madame Sorel—that was the dressmaker's name—was obviously quite confused when Nielsen asked her about Miss Derry, and evidently didn't know what her client demanded of her in such an unexpected circumstance.

So, Nielsen left his card and begged Miss Derry to write to him as soon as his visit would suit her.

And with that, he went away.

Miss Derry, however, had no such desire. She wrote him a card in which she told him very politely that she had just received news from Major Johnson, and now asked Mr. Nielsen and his friend to regard her visit to Cranbourne Grove as not having happened.

"That's certainly a lie," said Nielsen.

The doctor laughed. "So now the tables have turned back in favor of the Throgmorton party!"

"No," Nielsen said, "not really. But you know, Mr. Derry is a well-known and respected man. If the daughter doesn't want to approach us, I'll just go and visit her father."

"I have no objection to that," said the doctor thoughtfully, "but then I would take the cat and the collar with me. We must find out at any cost if 'Amy's Puss' really belongs to *this* Amy, for there is, of course, the possibility that the other lady involved in this tragedy will also be Amy."

Nielsen ordered a coach and put Amy's Puss in a basket; the cat wailed for a little while, but she soon succumbed to the inevitable. Mr. Derry's address was easy to locate: he was an important businessman and lived on the north side of the park.

At three o'clock in the afternoon, Nielsen's coach drove up to a beautiful, large house on Westbourne Terrace.

Mr. Nielsen asked for Miss Derry. Miss Derry was not at home.

Then he asked about Mrs. Derry, and she was at home.

When she appeared, Nielsen gave her the cat with a bow.

"Oh, is it possible? That's Amy's cat!" she cried in astonishment.

31

Nielsen showed no surprise.

"Where in the world did you find the cat?" inquired the dignified elderly lady after exchanging friendly greetings with the animal.

"In Cranbourne Grove Number 48, where I live," Nielsen said.

The lady clasped her hands in astonishment.

"So, the pussy went miles through Kensington Garden? But if so, how in the world did you, a stranger, know that the cat belonged here?"

Nielsen hesitated. The good old lady didn't seem to know about Cranbourne Grove 48. But she had to be familiar with the name of the major, if he and Amy had really had a serious relationship. He said, "Of course, that is quite extraordinary; but the house where I live belongs to Major James Johnson."

The lady turned pale. "Major Johnson," she repeated after a pause. "I don't know, Mr. . . . ."

"Nielsen," he finished.

"Mr. Nielsen, whoever you are. And I know Major Johnson almost as little as I know you. It is unlikely we will meet again, Mr. Nielsen, and you understand that I can't talk to a stranger about family business. And I don't advise you to talk about it with my husband. Not at all. On the contrary, I have to ask you to leave. Do you hear me? I must ask you to leave."

It looked as if Mrs. Derry feared that someone—no doubt her husband—might join their conversation.

"I can only assure you," she added, "that since Major Johnson left the army last fall, neither I nor my husband know anything about him, and if Amy's cat was found in his house, that can only be explained one way, that he simply stole the cat—But please excuse me. I expect my husband."

Nielsen could not stay longer if he didn't want to be intrusive. So, he got up and left.

But the cat stayed behind.

***

The doctor rubbed his hands in pleasure, "Question one is done. Amy's cat is really Amy's cat. We now need to keep a close eye on the Derry family, especially on this Amy whose life's work seems to be promising the blue from the sky. I think we now have every reason to return to her and her love affair, and we must also try to get to know more about the major. We already know that he's a cat thief."

***

Late in the afternoon, a messenger boy came carrying a basket—in it slept the cat. There was also a letter written in fine script—not that of the note the doctor had found. It was signed by Amy Derry and read,

"The cat's collar did once belong to me; I have reason to believe that it was stolen from me. The cat, on the other hand, doesn't belong to me, so I am sending it back." —Nothing else.

The doctor scratched his head. "Now we have the cat again, Nielsen. At least for the moment, we shall have to abandon our efforts to find our way through our famous Amy's lies. But that's no reason to treat her cat any worse."

Chapter Ten

"Nielsen," said the doctor the next morning after breakfast, "we've come so far now that it's time to devise a proper battle plan. We must ask ourselves what the police in our place would do now. And I mean, this Amy, after so many lies—big and small—made herself so suspicious that the police would undoubtedly bring her in. But let's not forget that Amy doesn't need to reveal the truth to us and we can't arrest her either. Nevertheless, we must subject her to a very serious and sharp interrogation. Let us exercise your brain and plan a masterstroke."

Nielsen smiled. "It's already done, esteemed Doctor. Of course, Miss Derry has no obligation to tell us the truth, but she will certainly shy away from us causing her more trouble. And with the help of her fear, we will succeed in getting everything we want from her. This is a simple police trick. But to be able to strike, we must have weapons, and these weapons we will get from another source. Mr. Armstrong is our man. We need to know the whole history of this business, and we can only get to know that from Mr. Armstrong on the one hand and Miss Derry on the other. We must interrogate them separately."

"And how are you going to make Armstrong talk? By an appeal to his better angels?"

"No," said Nielsen with a grin, "but not five houses away from Armstrong lives a Mr. Davis, who is also a house agent. These two gentlemen are competitors, and that says it all!"

"Excellent!" laughed the doctor. "You go to Mr. Davis and complain about how dissatisfied you are with Armstrong. And if you promise Davis good business, then, no doubt, he'll open the floodgates of his eloquence, and you'll learn more than enough about Armstrong to drive him into a corner."

Nielsen rubbed his hands.

"I'm going. And when I have drained Armstrong to the dregs, armed with this information, I will go to Miss Derry and force her to come out with the truth. We will then be able to exchange the undefined places around our current location for a better map of the area."

"Good," agreed the doctor. "I'm going to make a sketch of Turner's immortal *Snow Storm*. I still remember a donkey masquerading as a professor in Copenhagen, who called this wonderful painting "a head-cold" and a "sneezing stimulant." Such a scoundrel! I wish I had him and all his colleagues down in the lime with our Mister X!"

This was a matter that Nielsen never argued about with the doctor. Everyone has the right to ride his hobby horse if he does so only within his own four walls—

Nielsen went to see Mr. Davis, who lived five houses away from Armstrong, and lamented over the estate agent's shortcomings. Mr. Davis regretted that an unkind fate had brought Mr. Nielsen together with this—to use a milder word—con artist, and when Nielsen wished to know more, the agent said diplomatically that Mr. Armstrong's reputation was by no means the best. He was involved in an affair regarding a construction company, which had brought heavy losses to several well-respected people. Among the speculators even an officer— a certain Major Johnson—was to be found, and he had been forced by this affair to take his leave from the army. It was a real scandal, and as for the main parties of the affair, one need look no further than Mr. Armstrong and, besides him, a certain Mr. Weston, who was particularly notorious.

Nielsen wished to find out more, but the worthy Mr. Davis didn't know anything else; he knew the gossip but not the details.

Thus, Nielsen parted on the friendliest terms with his new acquaintance, his wallet full of addresses, which he didn't need. He was a little disappointed with the yield of his visit, but he believed, nonetheless, that he could use what knowledge he had acquired to corner Mr. Armstrong.

And it wasn't long until he sat, earnest and reserved, in Mr. Armstrong's private office, not unlike Rhadamanthus, the judge of the dead in Greek legend.

"Sir," he began in a dignified tone, "when I came to you before, I did so with the intention of establishing business relations with a man who had his business in a neighborhood like this. Though I had just met you, I trusted you and I took the house you recommended, although it was too expensive for me. But we liked it, and trusting you, Mr. Armstrong, my friend and I moved in."

Mr. Armstrong shifted uneasily in his chair; he didn't quite know where this was all leading.

Nielsen continued, "I'm not just anybody off the street, I'm a lawyer by profession. And as such, my job brings me together with highly respected people to whom I must give my current address . . ."

Armstrong interrupted him, "Oh, the street in which you live is considered elegant."

"Let me finish," snapped Nielsen, "I am not speaking of the street, nor of the house, but of its owner. Major Johnson has been dismissed from the army for some dirty business, hasn't he? Mr. Weston and probably Mr. Throgmorton are downright infamous for the same reason, correct? And finally, you, Mr. Armstrong—this affair with the construction company . . ."

Armstrong roared, "I will not sit here and be insulted!"

Nielsen looked at him sharply, "Stay calm, Mr. Armstrong, everyone knows about the affair. I don't care what kind of people own the house, but if I'm plagued and molested every single day because of the dubious business of these people, then I have the right to complain, and I am complaining. Especially to you, Mr. Armstrong. You told me nothing but lies when I rented the house. You told me it belonged to a major in the army; but you neglected to mention that this major had been expelled from the army for lying. You also pretended not to know the name of the former owner; but you staged this scandalous affair together with him—Do you think such behavior is honorable? Hardly. And I tell you, Mr. Armstrong, that I will not let you deceive me. I must insist that you tell me everything, or—on my honor—I will go straight to a lawyer and tell him the whole story. I have to be clear about who the rightful owner of the house really is, because I don't feel like paying my money and being thrown out one fine day because your swindlers have no right to the house."

Nielsen berated Mr. Armstrong in a loud voice, causing acute embarrassment to a number of potential clients waiting in the anteroom. Armstrong twisted and wriggled back and forth; he did not dare climb up on his high horse, for there was more than a little truth in Mr. Davis's gossip.

Perhaps, he decided, it would be better to tell the truth.

"What do you want to know?" he asked resignedly.

"Everything," said Nielsen, and Armstrong began.

The major, Armstrong admitted, was involved in the construction company, which was just an unfortunate speculation, nothing else. The major did resign his commission but for other reasons—strictly disciplinary. The house was owned by Mr. Throgmorton and his sister, Mrs. Weston, together. Armstrong cited the major as the owner only because Throgmorton and Weston had such ill-repute because of their business failures. That Weston was a drunkard and the major was courting his wife did nothing to improve matters. For this reason, the gentlemen found it right to leave England for some time, and they moved, for economic reasons, to a port on the west coast of Denmark. Whether or not Major Johnson had gone with them, Armstrong didn't know. But the major had always been very anxious to avoid the Derry family, and he had finally spread the rumor that he had gone to Burma. There might even be some truth in this, for Johnson had given Throgmorton authority to receive any monies or correspondence that might be sent to him. The power of attorney was dated April 30 of this year.

Nielsen interrupted him, "Well, you knew all this about these people, and then you told me something quite different."

The agent had no choice but to admit it.

"Do you know Miss Derry?" was Nielsen's next question.

"The young lady has been here once or twice in the last few days," Armstrong said, "but per my instructions, I have told her nothing. I received orders not to tell anyone anything."

"Well, Mr. Armstrong," said Nielsen, finally, in a gentler tone, "I am glad that you have now explained the matter to me. For your own sake, however, I would advise you not to share a word of this conversation with your former comrades; it would scarcely be to your advantage if you told these gentlemen that you have followed your better judgment and spoken freely to me. I don't want you to regret your sincerity. Misfortune can strike us all, and I want to believe that you have become a victim of circumstance. I'll stand by your side from now on, and I'm not, as I said, just anybody off the street—One more question, and then I'm done. When did you see the major for the last time?"

The agent rummaged among his papers.

"On April 26 he was here with Mr. Throgmorton. I haven't seen either of them since."

"And Mr. Weston?"

"I haven't seen Mr. Weston since mid-April. I rarely met with these gentlemen."

Nielsen went straight home; he was satisfied with his results.

"Doctor," he said, "now we progress. We know that Major Johnson obviously courted Mrs. Weston, that the major wished to disappear for some time, and that the other two men were anxious to make him disappear forever. This has all happened since the 26th of April. Further, we know that Weston and Throgmorton are most unpleasant people, that the house doesn't belong to the major, and that he has authorized Throgmorton to receive his money."

The doctor nodded, "That leads us to believe that during the period between April 26th and 29th the two swindlers murdered the major and then moved out of the country. For unknown reasons they traveled to a Danish fishing village. Well, we will find them there. But the cat—Amy's cat? If Miss Derry is right—if the cat doesn't belong to her and she has nothing to do with this drama—why did she tell us so many lies? Why did she say, for example, that she knows the major's address, whereas in reality she has no idea? What does she still want from him?"

"My next task is to find out all of this. And after the good results I have achieved with Mr. Armstrong, I am less perplexed about how I can achieve something with this young lady. The real difficulty is more in gaining access to her. And, of course, after this news from Armstrong, I am willing to treat her with all care."

The doctor put his head on the side.

"Are you then convinced again of her innocence? The unfavorable news about Throgmorton and Weston doesn't prove that. Bear in mind that Miss Amy Derry may have been in cahoots with these gentlemen, and, driven to despair by the major's two-timing, she took jealous, bloody revenge on the faithless major in this very house, while the two scoundrels, Throgmorton and Weston, used her actions for their pecuniary enrichment. I tell you, if the girl has completely clean hands, she'll tell you what she knows. You don't even have to threaten her."

"And if she doesn't have clean hands?" Nielsen asked.

"Then let's hope we'll find the key to unlock the riddle in her and save ourselves a trip to Hjørring."

***

Nielsen made his way to Clarendon Road, but Madame Sorel, now having received her instructions, was unwilling to receive him.

Nielsen left his visiting card behind.

Dear Miss! It is useless to reject my visit. I know where Major Johnson is; maybe you are interested in that. By the way, *you* began our acquaintance: you came to me, and I would rather settle this matter with you than with your father. That's why I'll be back here tomorrow morning at eleven o'clock. Yours faithfully . . .

A favorable response arrived that same evening in the form of a telegram.

Chapter Eleven

It was a bright, fresh morning when Nielsen took the train to Notting Hill Gate. Everyone looked happy and cheerful, only Nielsen could not enjoy spring's reawakening of nature and the sunshine flooding everything. When the train slid underground, this environment, with its dark walls and tunnels, seemed to suit his mood best. He just could not take pleasure in imposing himself on a young woman or in gaining her confidence through threats. However, he came to her with good intentions; he didn't believe in her guilt; sparing her was exactly what he wished, and he hoped she would emerge from the conversation without discord. She, the innocent, might only help him find the culprit.

When he returned to the light of day and walked beneath the green trees of Holland Park Street with its lush gardens on both sides, a sense of freedom and relief came over him. The pleasure in the awakened spring began to fill him, and he thought how he must communicate that feeling to her. He wanted to win her trust without threats, for she, a young woman, would already give him, a young man, the easy confidence that accompanies all youth.

The house was hidden behind trees in a row with other beautiful villas. Nielsen was admitted and found Miss Derry. She stood there tall and elegant, in a new, tight-fitting spring outfit with a small, bright, flower-decked straw hat on her head.

She greeted him politely, but rather coolly, and asked him to sit down.

He now spoke of the purpose of his visit, and as he spoke, he saw that her mouth tightened and her eyes sharpened; he saw, without understanding why, that this would be a hard fight.

And after he had spoken, she said in a clear, steady voice, "It can't surprise you, Mr. Nielsen, that I can't or don't want to trust you—a complete stranger. You know—as you have interfered—you know that I was engaged to Major Johnson. You also know that the engagement was cancelled, that it happened at the request of my relatives . . ."

Nielsen interrupted her.

40

"And I know you don't see the matter in this light! You must remember, Miss Derry, that you came to me first when you asked me to give you the letters for the major. So, I didn't visit you first, I didn't know anything about you until you came to me. And now I have reason to ask for a full explanation."

"By what right?" she asked, almost hoarsely.

"By the ordinary right of being a fellow human," he replied. "We don't stand alone here on earth, other paths are constantly crossing ours, and our interests are easily stirred. The simple instinct of self-preservation—a strong, innate instinct—causes us, when our paths have crossed with those of others, to ask what has caused the encounter. I must tell you: a week ago, the names Derry and Johnson didn't mean anything to me; but now these names have caught my interest. I know that they are connected with a crime that, I suspect, has been committed."

Miss Derry went pale.

"Yes, with a crime," Nielsen continued, "and I want to get to the bottom of this crime. It is not in my nature to stand by idly, but to take any important thing in hand, as if it were mine. This Major Johnson is the center of a series of actions that may be called criminal. And as a citizen, I have the right to protect society from crime. That's why I'm sitting here waiting for your explanation."

"I don't understand what you mean," said Miss Derry in a trembling voice.

"Well, let me explain then. When I rented that house in Cranbourne Grove, I was told that it belonged to a major who had gone to Burma. That didn't concern me; I simply paid the rent to the agent. But then you came and asked me to send you any letters for the major. I promised you, but when I asked the agent about it, he protested strongly against it; He showed me a power of attorney that the major had given to another person and forbade me to comply with your request. We found in the apartment a brief note from you, Miss Derry—it *was* from you, correct? But you told us a falsehood, for you wished to get rid of us. The little episode with the cat who lived in the house wearing a silver collar with your name increased our suspicions against you. You tried to persuade me to act in your interests and to deceive your parents. The agent told me the major wished to disappear for a while. You claim to know where he is; I don't believe you though.

41

And I want to tell you what my opinion is: Major Johnson has fallen into the hands of two criminals who abuse his name, use his money for themselves, and even seek his life."

Miss Derry listened with open mouth until Nielsen had finished his long speech; then she sank back, stricken.

Nielsen, who was watching her keenly, continued, "Now I ask you to openly answer some questions: Do you know where Major Johnson is? Do you know if it was his own free will that brought him into the hands of these men, Weston and Throgmorton? What do you know of his relationship with Mrs. Weston? And why did you want me to pass on the major's letters to you?"

"I must refuse to answer," she said firmly.

"Very well," said Nielsen, "I can't force you to. But perhaps you'll still regret that you didn't answer me—that is, when you face those who have the power to make you talk."

Then she got up and said proudly, "Your threats don't frighten me. Nothing happened between the major and myself that I should be ashamed of. I acted properly and will answer to God and, if necessary, to man. I'm not intimidated by threats."

"A just phrase," thought Nielsen, realizing he could achieve nothing this way. And he didn't want to mention the body in the cellar, at least not yet.

"Miss Derry," he said, changing his tone, "I don't wish to force you to answer. I am only looking out for your own interests. I have to see Major Johnson, I have to talk to him. Not about you; I'm not going to get involved in your relationship with him. I'm just asking you to tell me where he is."

"I don't know," was her short answer.

"Does that mean you don't want to tell me?"

She answered calmly and self-composed, "If I did know, I would not tell you. I don't trust you."

"Very well," said Nielsen, "if anything unpleasant happens to you now, don't forget that it is because of your own decisions. I don't wish to continue this conversation."

"Do you intend to go to my father?" she asked hoarsely. "Don't do that. You must not do that, I tell you! Because if you do, then . . . then I will take steps, and the blame for my fate will fall on you."

Her cheeks glowed and her chest heaved up and down with

agitation. He realized that she was a real British girl, full of fire and courage, that she meant what she said, and that she had a will; he had to be careful not to stretch her bow until it broke.

"I'm a gentleman," said Nielsen politely. "If you ask it, I will only deal with you, not your father. While you refuse to give me any information, I believe it is because you are not informed yourself. For if you knew something, it would be foolish to mislead me. You don't even know where the major is, but you'd give everything you own to find out."

Her face remained unmoved; she stood tall as before.

"I promise you, Miss Derry, that you will be the first I tell when I have found the major—for I want to find him—alive or dead."

"Major Johnson is not dead," she said quietly.

"Would you have known if he was dead?" Nielsen asked indifferently.

She was silent.

"Just tell me *one* thing, just *one* thing: Have you spoken to this man since April 28 of this year?"

"Mr. Nielsen, "she replied in a firm voice," I see from your behavior that you are a spy for the police. You must excuse me saying so, but it is obvious. And I tell you, *I* will not turn the major over to the police, however badly he may have acted. If you want, you can arrest me; I could not care less."

Nielsen bowed.

"You're wrong, Miss Derry, I don't want to bother you or him. But I want to tell you one thing: you think the major left the country in the company of two suspicious people; I believe, on the other hand, he is still here in the country, helpless, wordless—in a word, murdered!"

"You are upsetting yourself in vain, Mr. Nielsen," she said quietly, "and you are wasting your time uselessly."

Nielsen felt the same way. "Well," he said, "then I'll write to you, as soon as I find him, whether in China or Peru, I'll definitely find him!"

She smiled bleakly.

"I don't know what your motivation for all this is—with me anyway—you must've already realized that—you are just wasting your time."

Nielsen bowed and left.

Chapter Twelve

"You didn't get away with it as easily as you did with Mr. Armstrong," Koldby said with a laugh as Nielsen finished his report. "Amy was too much for you! Oh, good Nielsen, I'm beginning to believe that you'll be shipwrecked by this affair—stranded on the sandbar of femininity! Shame on you—you, a big, strong fellow! Can't you see she did it? That she has his murder on her conscience? What else would seal her lips so tightly?"

"I don't think so," said Nielsen, hunched over a shipping timetable. "The Esbjerg steamer leaves tomorrow. I suggest, Doctor, we go to Hjørring and see what we can get out of the others."

"And in the meantime, Amy's running away," mocked the doctor. "Just playing you for a fool, hee, hee!"

"Oh, no!" said Nielsen, slamming the timetable shut. "If she wanted to run away, she would have done so long ago. I believe in her innocence. She looked honorable."

"Yes, very honorable, especially when she was lying!"

"If she lied, she did it with conviction. It was just female delicacy in her. She didn't want to trust a stranger. Because she loves this major, whoever and whatever he is, she has forgiven him—in short, she longs for him—and he, he is lying in our cellar coated in lime."

The doctor mumbled, "Unless her certainty is due simply to her knowing that he is perfectly well. You say with determination that the major is the man in the cellar. How do you know *that*?"

"He must be, Doctor. Remember, he has given a questionable person a power of attorney authorizing him to receive his letters and money. Yes, what sensible person does such nonsense? What possible entertainment could he derive from having these two swindlers steal his money? What advantage would it give him to disappear from London and even from England? He is not wanted by the police, and if he wants to avoid Miss Derry, he could do so with ease, even staying in London. And on the other hand, it is very probable that these two, Weston and Throgmorton, wanted him dead to acquire his fortune."

"All very possible," said the doctor. "But why didn't you tell this to

44

Miss Derry?"

"Simple, because I don't know if she's the culprit. I mean the one who pushed the blade in . . . nothing else, even though the other two benefit from the deed. If this is the case, then we should probably decide against Miss Derry—but if so, I confess I have no wish to do so. I like the girl; she is brave, determined, and active."

"And beautiful."

"And beautiful. And if she stabbed the major she had a good reason for doing so. All we can do now is to go to Denmark and tell these gentlemen that they have been discovered and they may be dealing with the London police."

"And the cat and Madame Sivertsen?" the doctor asked.

"They stay here. I will take on the expenses myself, unless you want to share them with me. If we then come to a conclusion later that causes us to drop the matter—that is, if Miss Derry really did the deed, then we'll call Madame Sivertsen home and put the cat at the disposal of Miss Derry."

"And if the cat belongs to the other lady? You forget that there are two ladies involved here."

Nielsen smiled, "Oh no! I only know one, Doctor. She is already enough for me. All I've gotten to know from her is that she acted rightfully in every instance, that is, without any malicious intent. I don't think he was worth much, our man in the cellar; he doesn't interest me much anymore. But one thing is certain: The puzzle must be solved!"

The doctor said nothing, but they did what Nielsen had suggested and left London the next evening. And as they stood on deck of the Esbjerg steamer and watched the lights of Harwich vanish in the distance, the doctor said almost mockingly, "Our visit didn't last long."

"Please." replied Nielsen. "We don't know whether or not we will have to return soon. As it stands, at the moment, we know nothing at all."

"Do you think," asked the doctor, "that the police would have achieved more if they were in our place? If so, then we haven't been particularly blessed with success."

Nielsen shook his head.

"Nevertheless, we have done well," he said. "Mr. Armstrong for example, if the police had acted on our behalf, he might well be cooling his heels on the floor of an interrogation room. Miss Derry would be even worse off—maybe even dead. And the trio we're about to visit now would have already fled the scene. No, Doctor, boasting is not normally my style, but I must openly confess that, by taking matters into our hands, we have been of benefit to all."

"Especially to ourselves," said the doctor, laughing. "Because the first people who would have been imprisoned would have surely been—us! By the way, if the events bring us back to London, that might still happen. So, we have every reason to be happy now, but to be careful later."

***

The sea was calm and the sky clear. The doctor sat on deck all day painting the water. Nielsen leaned against the railing and looked at the small frothy waves; but his thoughts were far away —with the riddle he wanted to solve, although the wide, open water reduced it to something insignificant, abstract; it was a matter that touched the intellect, but not the soul.

Nielsen was still young, and Amy—the Amy of the affair—too impersonal.

And while the ship steamed toward Denmark, Madame Sivertsen sat in her chamber behind the kitchen in Cranbourne Grove with Amy's cat, and in the cellar the dead man lay quiet and still.

Part 2
In Løkken

Chapter One

Not far from the Bay of Sorrow lies Løkken, friendly and inviting with its two small church towers and the large red-painted maritime sign—a small fishing village between sandy dunes.

It was here that Holger Nielsen and Doctor Koldby hoped to unravel the mystery of Cranbourne Grove.

Mr. Armstrong, of course, had given them the address "General Delivery, Hjørring," but in Hjørring the postman told them that an Englishman bearing the name they mentioned had been living in Løkken since the beginning of May, and so the two partners in justice took a coach to Løkken.

As they passed the hills near Børglum on their journey, Nielsen ordered the coach to stop and they got out. Because Børglum Hill with its abbey of the same name, is one of the most beautiful places in Denmark. The sun was high, and a stiff breeze was blowing from the sea. Nielsen inhaled the delightfully fresh air and exclaimed to his companion, "In this clear air any concealment must be impossible. See how the sun shines on the blue water! And if the land doesn't help us, then we call the sea—the sea there in the west."

The doctor nodded, "Of course it is more beautiful here than in London. The air is clearer; in London, you literally gasp like a fish on dry land. At home it's always most beautiful. And you know what? Why don't we leave this whole affair to itself, call Madame Sivertsen home, and turn the remainder of our lease over to Amy's cat?"

Nielsen turned and walked back to the coach.

"No sentimentalities, Doctor. We have a duty to fulfill, let's get down to business!"

The descent from the Børglum Hill was slow; the road was sandy and difficult, and the horses heavy and sluggish. And, after all, the coachman was a true Jutlander who took his time.

"What is actually your plan?" the doctor asked.

"For the time being, I haven't decided on anything in particular—unless it's just to explore. But look, Doctor!"

Doctor Koldby glanced over the front seat of the coach and saw, some distance ahead of them, a lady on a two-wheeler who had apparently lost control of her bicycle. She swayed to the left and then to the right, and, suddenly, she lay in the ditch. Two gentlemen, who evidently belonged to her, were riding bikes behind the coach but overtook it at the point where the road made a sharp bend. They stopped at the scene of the accident and jumped off.

The coach stopped too.

The lady sat pale and apparently with aching limbs on the edge of the trench; she held her left wrist with her right hand.

Nielsen jumped out of the coach, and the doctor, too, climbed out, albeit more deliberately, and then approached the lady and her companions.

"*Impossible*," they heard one of the latter say, "*quite impossible*."

"Englishmen," whispered the doctor.

Nielsen lifted his hat and asked politely if he could help; he said it in English and was immediately welcomed. The two English gentlemen were even more welcoming when the doctor introduced himself as a doctor. The lady had sprained her wrist and was unable to continue the journey, especially since the front wheel of her bicycle was now damaged. After the doctor had put a wet compress on her, that is, a handkerchief dipped in a puddle of water, she was given a seat in their carriage while the bike was placed across the other seat.

The gentlemen introduced themselves as Mr. Weston and Mr. Throgmorton from London, while the lady was Throgmorton's sister, Mrs. Weston.

Doctor Koldby accepted the introduction very coolly, while Nielsen blushed with joy.

The three were the people from Cranbourne Grove; only the murdered man was missing, which only justified the assumption that he would be Johnson.

When they arrived at their destination, Mrs. Weston, despite her pain, expressed her gratitude to the two, while the gentlemen assured them that only a higher power could have led the two friends to Løkken.

Then Mrs. Weston was put to bed, and they sent for the local doctor, because Koldby didn't want to trespass on a colleague's territory.

When the two friends later stood in their hotel room, the doctor said, "I know what you think now, Nielsen."

"Well, what?"

"I know that look! You think she's innocent! Yes—and Miss Derry's stock is starting to decline again. But nonetheless—our initial effort here has not been too bad. So far, I've always thought such coincidences occurred only in the imagination of timid novelists, but today I have seen that sometimes life can have its romantic moments as well. And I almost begin to believe that a higher power must have brought us together so quickly with our murderers."

Nielsen shook his head and replied, "You know, Doctor, we must abstain from all biased opinions."

"Pfft. We confront each other's biases regularly," said the doctor. "You forget it especially when the suspects turn out to be female and young and lovely. Thank your lucky stars that you've got such an elderly, illusion-free, women-hater with you as I. But I would like to say one more thing, I hope that this lady here is not named Amy as well. If so, I must protest. Even timid novelists must have limits."

"Silence!" said Nielsen—for at that moment the two Englishmen walked past their window, and one of them said, "The doctor thinks Amy will be restored in a few days."

Nielsen and Doctor Koldby stared at each other in incredulous silence. They each had but one thought—the cat, and Koldby finally said, "Nielsen, it appears we should have packed our mouse catcher and brought her to Løkken."

Chapter Two

The beach at Løkken runs wide, white, and flat. Sand, nothing but sand, forming long, low dunes, only now and then covered with seaweed.

The dunes haven't always been there; for the boatmen of Løkken remember from their childhood when they used to sail to Norway on their fathers' ships, that Løkken was the stockyard for Hjørring. Some of the warehouses from that time are still preserved, standing among the straw-colored cabins of the fishermen and looking out over the bay. And this is how Løkken must have looked when the English dropped anchor in the bay in 1801 and poured heavy cannonballs onto the city. Løkken is no longer exposed to this danger, because the wide dunes now keep it hidden from the sea.

Actually, Løkken is nothing but a fishing village of a few hundred souls, but in the summer numerous tourists come to this lovely place. For when the bay lies in graceful clarity, when the sun with its rays makes the Rubjerg cliffs, which rise steeply in the north from the sea, and the long bank, which extends to the south to the steep slope of Borbjerg, shine in bright summer light, then Løkken can be compared with the shores of the Mediterranean.

This is how Løkken looked today, graceful and bathed in sunlight.

The tourists dozed comfortably in their beach chairs while the children played and dug in the sand below. A little way down from this spot, the tourists joked and laughed in the shallow, balmy water, and farther down, one saw fishermen, serious and busy with their cutters and motorboats, as if there were no holidays for them, and they had nothing to do with the sunny side of life.

Nielsen, too, had settled here in a beach chair; he was in a conversation with Mrs. Weston, who now had recovered from the accident and was able to use her hand as usual; they had already become acquainted.

Mrs. Weston was beautiful and slender, with deep black hair and eyes. Her oval face was a little pale, but her complexion was clean and smooth. She herself spoke little, but evidently loved to have a young

51

man around who would talk to her, and Nielsen spoke English well and fluently.

Meanwhile, the two Englishmen ran around on the beach; they would have liked to go sailing, but such things were not a custom in Løkken. From time to time they would sail out with the fishermen to look for mackerels unless they were on a bicycle ride or on a walk along the beach in the sharp westerly wind.

Mrs. Weston didn't talk to them much; a strange irritable look always came to her large dark eyes, when her husband turned to her, and she didn't seem to like her brother at all. The latter was obviously the leader; he made all arrangements with the landlord, and gave orders to the other two in short, sharp tones, which they apparently obeyed. He was short and stocky, quite unlike his sister, though he had dark hair like her. He was pockmarked and had piercing gray eyes that always looked displeased and unfriendly. Everyone avoided him, and the landlord complained of his stinginess and rudeness. Mr. Weston, on the other hand, was harmless, tall, thin, and boring. He seemed to rave about his wife, even though she treated him so rudely. They didn't live together like a married couple, but instead had separate rooms in the hotel.

The whole of Løkken talked about the English guests. Nobody knew where they had come from. They themselves didn't say anything, and Nielsen could not get anything out of them either.

The owner of the hotel reported that they had arrived very early, even before the season's opening, that they paid on time and seemed to be wealthy. They received few letters and kept themselves separate from the other guests. The event that had brought them together with Nielsen and Koldby had been the first time the English had a reason to communicate with other tourists. Since they had arrived earlier in the season than other guests, they had their seats at the top of the table and had already made themselves at home there.

The other guests—mostly merchants from the cities of East Jutland—regarded them with suspicion and stayed away. For some reason, Nielsen and Koldby were also regarded as Englishmen, and the cool behavior displayed to the English was, quite unfairly, also transferred to them.

Nielsen was all right with it. Without having a definite plan, he spent time in Mrs. Weston's company, noticing that she liked him. Of course, she didn't trust him, and she never spoke of herself. But Nielsen could still perceive that she longed for England, and that the company of her two companions was troublesome to her; she seemed to despise her husband and even abhor her brother. This brother evidently had power over her; that was clear, and it fit into Nielsen's view of the Cranbourne Grove affair. He had not yet conceived any clear plan; as things lay, there was currently nothing to achieve. He first had to win her friendship, then, if possible, her trust, in order to go from his formless and indefinite suspicions to knowledge. Of course, that was not very honorable, but he had no other means to reach his goal.

"Mrs. Weston, "said Nielsen," how did you come to choose this side of the North Sea for your stay? There are plenty of seaside resorts in England, and you don't seem to care much for this country and its people."

She shook her head, "One is not always master of one's actions, Mr. Nielsen. I have to spend this summer by the sea for the sake of my nerves; it is cheaper here than in England, and besides—my brother and my spouse wished to live here for a while. And, so, here I am."

"You'd rather not be here?" Nielsen asked.

She looked up with a tired smile.

"I have so few wishes—none at all. I'm just tired—I long for peace. I prefer to sit quietly and look over the sea, which murmurs so pleasantly here. I also like to listen to you; you speak so calmly and nicely. It is only when you ask questions that I don't like to listen to you. I never ask questions, and there is so much to talk about besides us. You can talk about art—about music—books."

Nielsen shrugged, "But I prefer to talk about people, of men and women and—as you've already heard—of crime and guilt. It is my hobby, and it may bore you. But all in all, it is always people who are the most compelling to us. And when I talk to you, Mrs. Weston, I would very much like to know who and what you are."

"That's a funny way of expressing your curiosity, isn't it?" she smiled. "Who and *what* I am? I am nothing—nobody! But it is fine for you to speak about guilt and crime; I'm also interested in that, especially when you talk about it. Yesterday, your friend, Doctor Koldby, told me you denied that there was such a thing as crime. And that you also may not think that there are bad people, correct?"

He shrugged.

"That depends on what you mean by bad people."

"Well, I mean, for example, a person who doesn't shy away from any action, no matter how evil it is, if it is to his advantage. Or a man who destroys the life of another, just to do evil to him . . . who takes pleasure in doing evil."

"I deny that such people exist at all," replied Nielsen. "This so-called wickedness is in my opinion nothing but a misunderstanding of the relationship between action and purpose. The best actions may seem bad if this relationship is ignored; but that a man would do evil for no reason, I don't believe that; there must always be a purpose, at least an imaginary advantage, that the person has for his actions. I believe, therefore, in erroneous calculations, but not in conscious wickedness."

Nielsen said this on purpose; he believed he knew what she was aiming for and tried to provoke her by contradiction.

"So, you don't believe in crimes and criminals?" she asked.

"In crimes, yes—but as far as the criminals are concerned, my view of them differs from that of the more popular opinion. In fact, I understand criminals to be individuals who, because of a lack of means of subsistence, lead a parasitic existence to the detriment of the other members of society; they accomplish this through actions that don't involve actual work but bring benefits to them without offering any value. Crime is a social evil, but with more of an epidemic than an acute nature, and those criminals who appear the least dangerous, the little thieves and the vagrants, are the most dangerous because of their persistence."

She looked up and asked, "But what about the murderers?"

"Murder depends on the circumstances alone. It *can* of course be a crime to kill a man, but it doesn't *have* to be. In the war it is even considered heroic to kill as many people as possible. Even killing, like all actions, can be justified and unjustified; it depends entirely on the motives."

She drew figures in the sand with the parasol.

"The Bible tells us . . . ."

"Mrs. Weston," he interrupted, "let us leave the Bible aside. It has been abused too often already for us to apply it to our case. In short, my view is that we don't have the right to kill someone else except in self-defense. But if killing is also unlawful, it certainly doesn't need to be a crime; it is a crime only if it can be classified under the category of those parasitic acts that I spoke about."

Mrs. Weston looked up with a soft smile.

"You mean, then, that only vagabonds and poor people who are not inclined to work can commit murder as a crime? The others are allowed, correct?"

"I didn't say that. We were talking about criminals—bad people. And I'm just saying there are criminals, there are crimes, and there are actions that must not be condemned in themselves but must be explained based on their motives first, before they can be judged. If we found a new name for it, that would be the first step. First, you must judge the motives and then the crime. At the moment it is just the other way around. But of course, I shouldn't explain everything to you in such detail; I just wanted to give you the broad strokes. Because you seem to be interested in murder and murderers."

"Me?" she responded with animation. "Well, to be honest, I've gained some interest through reading newspapers and detective stories. Thankfully, most of us spend our entire lives without coming into contact with this sort of person. But I'm interested, it would interest anyone."

Nielsen had risen.

"Of course, everyone is interested. Personally, I have come into contact with a very strange murder case—I will tell you another time, not today. The case is most interesting and well suited to explain my basic views, which, of course, can't be better explained than by examples."

Mrs. Weston smiled, "You're right. Because, with all due respect to your eloquence, your theory of murder and murderers is not quite clear."

"I hope to make it clear to you," Nielsen replied. "It's my hobby, and I want to do my best to show you what I mean, you especially."

"Why especially me?" she asked.

"Because I take a deep interest in you, Mrs. Weston."

She rose.

"I believe it is time for lunch," she said.

They both approached the hotel along the narrow path dug through the dunes and protected by plantings from the drifting sand. Nielsen was now well aware that Mrs. Weston was living here against her will, that she was interested in murderers, and that her companions were

55

men who, for the sake of their own advantage, didn't shy away from evil.

"You didn't find out much," said the doctor, as he and Nielsen walked after lunch on the dunes farther afield. "But do you know, Nielsen, the whole hotel is already talking about you and the English lady. When I left you alone with this lady the first time, of course, I thought you would, as a social avenger does, ferret out the truth. But now this fat cloth merchant from Randers and his wife have whispered so much into my ears during lunch that I have begun to become suspicious. Nielsen, my boy, I hope, after you have so excellently begun this drama as an avenging angel of justice in true tragedic style, that you will not end it as a comic *Innamorato* in the operettic style. You know. Something like the singer, who carries his beloved in his arms into the water every morning to the scandal of the whole bathing community."

"You're joking, Doctor," said Nielsen. "After all, you're right that the murder itself takes a back seat after the distance we've traveled and becomes something quite abstract, which differs definitely from what it was in Cranbourne Grove, psychologically."

"And what do you prefer?" the doctor asked.

"This, no doubt!"

"Hmm, and what are you going to do?"

Nielsen stretched and looked across the sea into the distance, "I'll do anything the situation demands, Doctor—I'll let things come to me, and watch—watch until I can see clearly."

"And then?"

Nielsen turned and put his hand on the doctor's shoulder, "Then maybe I will close my eyes and see nothing at all."

"That's to say, you will send a short message to Mr. Armstrong and let Madame Sivertsen follow us without the cat, as I suggested last Tuesday. Well, Nielsen, I know that whatever you do will be done well, as long as you have honorable intentions and you don't sail under false colors. But one thing, I beg you to always think kindly of: in our dealings with Miss Derry, there is still one way out that I generally consider, when it comes to innocent young men and nice-looking girls, namely, that the masculine takes the feminine and runs away with it— on the other hand, here the feminine is already provided with a quite legitimate spouse, which makes the case considerably more

56

complicated."

"I haven't the slightest intention of explaining myself," said Nielsen, reddening. "Not at least until we know a lot more than we do now."

"That's also right," agreed the doctor, "especially since we know next to nothing at the moment."

"Very true, my dear Doctor, then we agree."

"As always," said the latter, adding, "at least, as always when your thoughts are reasonable."

"The situation now is as follows," continued the doctor after a few moments of thoughtful silence. "The family gathered here, to whom providence introduced us in its unfathomable way, is indeed our trio from Cranbourne Grove. Mr. Weston is married to Mrs. Weston; he is tall, lean, and looks like a real fool, but we can hardly call him an idiot; at worst, he is of weak character. As for the lady, I shall withhold judgment until she is completely restored. But her brother— Throgmorton, is just made to be suspected. None of the external signs are missing: squinting eyes, connected eyebrows, and flat-fitting ears. In short, he looks so suspicious that my suspicion has already half become conviction.

"Just at the point in time we would have expected, the company arrived here. The address they gave Armstrong tells us that they already knew this area but were undecided whether to go to Løkken, Lønstrup, or Hirtshals. Mrs. Weston had already been to Lønstrup several years ago, as I have heard, as Miss Throgmorton accompanied by an elderly lady. Now they have chosen Løkken, where none of them had been before . . . What are you thinking now?"

"I think of Miss Amy Derry," said Nielsen.

"Ah!—You are probably making comparisons, right?—Well, which of the two Amys do you prefer?"

"This one definitely," replied Nielsen. "She is very lovely."

"That's what I said the first time we saw her. Poor Miss Derry! In the end, she's the killer, eh? And these staid folks here have nothing to do with the business, despite their suspicious behavior and Mr. Throgmorton's criminal appearance?! Ha! Ha! Ha!"

Chapter Three

The days went by, the sea remained calm and captivating, and the sun sent its warm rays over everything. Visitors came and went, Doctor Koldby walked and painted, and Nielsen lounged on the beach— usually accompanied by Mrs. Weston. The Englishmen were angry about it; but they said nothing, and sought distraction in sport, while the other tourists ignored Nielsen and his companion.

However, what good did it do—Nielsen didn't get anywhere, and he could not defend himself against the doctor's teasing comments. They had not heard from Miss Derry, and Madame Sivertsen's reports were only brief. The latter could not understand why the two gentlemen actually kept the expensive house in London. The cat, she wrote, had become round and fat; they had become friends by now—maybe the gentlemen had rented the house just for the cat?

The doctor also found the price a little expensive, and Nielsen had to admit that it was not a worthwhile investment. But worst of all, they didn't make the slightest progress. At last, the doctor decided to lend a hand and, in turn, to bring himself closer to the Englishmen. He rented a so-called fishing smack from an old fisherman named Silius Hansen and invited the Englishmen out sailing. The Englishmen went out with him once, but they soon found another fisherman north of the city, who was also ready to lend his vessel, and they went off alone on the sea.

One evening, when Nielsen and the doctor had lit their last cigars, Koldby revealed his heart to Nielsen.

"Look, Nielsen," he said, "we have now come to the point where a good general must make a decision. I suspect that you haven't yet succeeded in warming Mrs. Weston to the melting point. So, hurry up a bit, my dear man. I can tell that she is mortally wounded by her husband, and that she is happy dealing with you, my friend. So, ensure she is your ally completely and then proceed to attack. Of course, I suppose she is white as snow."

Nielsen shook his head. "That's not the way I'd rather work. No, let us direct our attack against the fortress where it looks strongest."

"Aha!" laughed the doctor, "you are a hero!"

"Yes, or a knight," said Nielsen. "It will certainly cause these gentlemen disgust, but we will force them to draw their weapons. And I'll let myself hang if we don't succeed. I will lure them with Jens Laursen's fishing boat 'Betty' far out on the sea—to the great sandbanks, and then, where they can't avoid me, I will open fire against them. What do you say?"

"Well, not bad," said the doctor, "but you'd better take only one of them. I'll hang on to Throgmorton while you go out with Laursen's Betty and take Weston with you alone."

"Well, you're right," Nielsen agreed. "So, you take Throgmorton as I sail out with Weston and do the inevitable."

"The inevitable? Do you want to tell him everything?"

"Yes."

"Would that be wise?"

"Well, listen to my whole plan. When we're at sea, I will tell Mr. Weston that I approached his wife and tried to entertain her. I don't want to offend his rights, but his wife interests me in the highest degree, for a lady of my acquaintance, whom he undoubtedly also knows, Miss Derry —"

"Ah! "interrupted the doctor.

"—Yes, now I'm playing off Miss Derry. Miss Derry, I say, told me that her fiancé, a certain Major Johnson, lost his heart to Mrs. Weston and broke the engagement. Of course, that will not excite him very much. But then I will go further. I say that Miss Derry doesn't want to give up her major, and that I have come to Løkken to find him. Of course, that also will not upset him much, because he knows well that the major is lying quietly in the cellar and is not so easy to find; he will probably laugh at me inwardly and explain outwardly that he doesn't understand a word of it. But these have been merely feints. Now I will launch my attack. I will say, 'Mr. Weston, it doesn't help you to play with me. We rented your house, Cranbourne Grove 48'—and—"

The doctor could no longer master himself. "—and down in the cellar we found . . . right?"

"May I call you a madman, Doctor, without offending you?"

"Certainly. Be my guest, for I can't be more slow-witted than you are now."

"Okay, so I call you a madman. Do you really think that I will say that to Weston? Thank God, I'm not the idiot you think I am. You should have a higher opinion of me after our long acquaintance."

"Nielsen," replied the doctor, "there is only a small step between excessive wisdom and insanity, and now you seem to want to be excessively wise."

"Are you able to listen to me quietly for two minutes?"

The doctor was, and Nielsen went on, "I say to my Englishman out there on the blue sea, 'If you don't come out with the pure truth, Mr. Weston, then I'll go back to London right away, and if I must rip open the floor in every single room in the house at Cranbourne Grove 48, I will do so, because I *want* to find the major—alive or dead!'—Well, what do you say now?"

The doctor bowed deeply and emptied his glass. "That's the right thing, really. Do that."

Several minutes went by in silence; Nielsen enjoyed his triumph while the doctor, with his finger to his nose, eagerly pondered. It stung him that Nielsen had bested him.

"What then?" he asked.

Nielsen smiled. "Of course, it is difficult to foresee what effect my words will have on my victim. But we must present a hypothesis."

"Wait a bit," said the doctor with a malicious laugh. "You are unbeatable. You expressed yourself so viciously clever that I had no answer. But now I have one. We know, of course, what Miss Derry has told us, but we also know that that lady, to put it mildly, doesn't take the truth very seriously. So, if Miss Derry herself has the major's death on her conscience, if she killed him out of jealousy and covered him in lime—in short, if she's the killer, then Mr. Weston will have every reason to look down on you from the moral high ground, and you would sink from the proud position of prosecutor into the questionable one of co-suspect."

"You forget that in your version, Mr. Weston won't know what's lying in the cellar of the house on Cranbourne Grove, and then, at worst, thinks I'm an idiot, which I gladly allow him to do. But in that case, our mission would also be at an end."

The doctor thought. "That is not entirely wrong," he said. "In that case we would again advance against Miss Derry and make valuable inquiries about her from the three English. I admit that. But now, supposing Mr. Weston is one of the killers, then . . ."

"Then my hypothesis shows its advantage," interrupted Nielsen. "Mr. Weston's first thought will be to flee to Throgmorton, but this will be prevented by the full length of the intervening bay. We are miles away from the coast, Throgmorton is not at hand, and I'm heading straight for my goal. Mr. Weston will be anxious and say a lot of things that we can't guess, but I'll listen very carefully. In the meantime, you talk in a similar way to Throgmorton—you just don't need to say anything about tearing open the floorboards. After our return, the two gentlemen will make plans on how best to escape—"

"Probably," said the doctor. "We have disturbed their summer stay anyway."

"I agree. But let me continue. At any rate, they will not want to travel without Mrs. Weston. We will then see how much she knows about the matter, and then devise our plan. No doubt she will not let these criminals carry her along. By this we have isolated the latter and . . . well, what should we anticipate so far, we will see what comes out in our inquiry, and then decide."

"It seems a good plan," said the doctor, "but in practice it will hardly be so smooth."

"Yes, that's because the whole thing is based on a hypothesis, my dear Doctor. But I'm tired of waiting. May it end as it pleases. Anyway, the time to act has come."

"Yes, you are right," said the doctor, and finished his drink.

The council of war was over.

Chapter Four

Jens Laursen was both a fisherman and a carpenter, a skinny man with a proper sailor's face. He was known in Løkken as one of the most excellent fishermen and was afraid of no weather; in the winter he caught more haddock than anyone, and in summer his lobster traps were always full.

Jens Laursen stood on the beach and made ready his "Betty." The "Betty" was the most beautiful boat in the whole harbor, large, wide-decked, and painted in gray and white; it was the only remaining sailboat in Løkken. All the rest had converted to engines. Jens had to rely on sailing, he would have to fish for a whole summer before he had saved the money for an engine.

"Petersen," Nielsen said to him—Petersen was Jens Laursen's father's name—"would you want to take me and another gentleman out tomorrow morning if the weather is fine?"

"With pleasure," said Jens, "is the other master the painter?"

"No, one of the Englishmen."

"That's fine. We'll sail at five o'clock, just after daybreak. The weather will be good, because the barometer is steady. So, come at five."

This half of the business was done, and now the other was left.

After lunch Nielsen suggested to Mr. Weston that they take a sailing trip together.

Mr. Weston hesitated and summoned his comrade.

Throgmorton could not stand Nielsen. Strangers were not pleasant to him at all. Besides, he was in a bad mood, probably as a result of a quarrel he had just had with his sister. Such disputes between the siblings, as people say, occurred quite frequently, and some claimed that Nielsen was the cause.

And Throgmorton took this opportunity to be quite ill-mannered.

"Sir," he said, "only coincidence has brought us together. You have rendered a service to my sister, which anyone else could have done. But you now make this service a pretext to impose your company on us. You have now become the cause of all sorts of talk about my sister.

62

You have put her reputation in danger. Yes, you have! Of course, I do not wish to make a fuss about it. What's done is done. But if your intention is now to throw yourself at my brother-in-law—perhaps to make up for what you have done badly with his wife—then I just want to tell you, take care of your own affairs and leave us alone. I'm sick of it now. As far as I'm concerned, you can go to hell."

It was not a very sociable response, and Nielsen flushed to the roots with anger. But he thought of his plans and replied politely, "I am convinced, Mr. Throgmorton, that you have no right to say that I have forced my company on anyone. I have talked to Mrs. Weston, whom I have the highest respect for, only because I thought she was pleased by it. Perhaps I was mistaken. But by no means am I willing to be insulted. Of course, I will talk to Mrs. Weston about it, and if anyone here should have allowed any innuendo, I will resolutely inquire after his name. I won't stand for any nonsense in such matters."

Throgmorton snorted, "I only wish that you leave *us*, my brother-in-law and me, alone. My sister is free to do whatever she pleases. Her husband will certainly preserve her honor."

"Certainly, I agree," said Nielsen peacefully. "But especially *your* behavior suggests the opposite. And for exactly the same reasons you just mentioned, I would like to spend a day with Mr. Weston, and I am convinced that in this way he and I will reach an understanding quickly and more pleasantly than by your rudeness. Because rude, you have been."

The two Englishmen consulted briefly, then Throgmorton said in the same tone, "I have no reason to change my tone or my words. I have given you my opinion freely, nothing else, and I ask you to do likewise."

Nielsen now looked at Mr. Weston, who in turn declared, "I agree with my brother-in-law. If I thought you dared to approach Mrs. Weston with bad intentions, I would act very differently toward you. I trust Mrs. Weston in every way. But regardless, I don't wish your acquaintance and ask you to take care of your own business."

And with that, Mr. Weston turned his back on Nielsen and walked off with a drooping posture.

Throgmorton followed him.

***

The doctor was painting in the middle of the dunes as Nielsen came slowly through the sand.

"Well?" he asked.

"Our plan fell into the water," said Nielsen. "Our two rotters were as rude as bears," and he told the doctor what had happened.

"Then our plan did fall into the water," said the doctor. "Now you'd like to take the scoundrels by the neck, eh?"

"Of course, I can't say that their behavior has made me warmer toward them. But after all, you must confess they are not so wrong to be suspicious of my intentions. So we will just have to change our tactics and think about it a little bit. We have time. Of course, the sailing trip tomorrow morning will not happen; I'll go down now and cancel the boat."

"Do that," said the doctor and returned to his work.

Nielsen went down to the beach, where he found Jens Laursen still busy with his "Betty."

"I will not be able to come with you tomorrow morning," he said.

"All right, all right," cried Jens happily, "the two Englishmen have spoken to me in the meanwhile. They offered me a good price for the boat, but since I had already promised you, I had to decline. So there is no need to apologize. I'll take the Englishmen out instead."

***

When Nielsen and Doctor Koldby were together again, the doctor smiled and asked him whether he would not now drop his knightly purpose and attack the fortress where it would appear weakest.

Nielsen was thoughtfully silent.

"My dear friend," continued the doctor, "I mean, there is nothing left for you. And remember what a favorable opportunity you will still have tomorrow: if our two rotters are out at sea, you may be able to uncover the whole story at a single blow—with *her* help. I would not leave such an opportunity unused. Good heavens—she's only a woman—and you, my friend, are really a genius!"

Nielsen didn't answer; he preferred to keep his thoughts to himself that evening.

And the doctor left him alone.

Chapter Five

It was during the afternoon of the following day that a strong wind set in and brought rain clouds up. Nielsen stood at the door of the hotel and nodded to the doctor who had just left his room.

"Now they've already hoisted up two signal balls at the marina," Nielsen said. "It is growing serious. Everyone is out at sea, and the wind is coming from the northwest. I think we'll see the lifeboat today."

The doctor rubbed his hands, "It's really fortunate that the Englishmen were so uncivilized yesterday. Otherwise, it would be you sitting out on the bay and rocking in Laursen's boat. You must agree that keeping the earth under your feet is always the most solid course!"

"I hope everything will be okay," Nielsen replied, shaking his head. "Fourteen motorboats are out there and four smacks and Betty with her sails. And all the men have families."

"Yes, and our two Englishmen too! If anything happens to Throgmorton and Weston, then the two Amys will be left behind and we may never get an explanation of our mystery. The storm might literally float our inquiry away."

"Doctor, how can you think of something like that? Come on, it's starting to pour, and the wind is racing through the trees, as if trying to uproot them. I think we'd do well to get to the lookout hill, and quickly."

They stepped out into the marketplace. In front of each door, they saw the occupants standing and looking out. The tourists from the hotel, wrapped in waterproof overcoats and scarves, struggled slowly forward against the storm. Down in the street it was rattling and clattering—all the wagoners were driving their horses home to be ready, if necessary, to drive the lifeboat out.

"Now they're hoisting up a third ball," cried the doctor, and indeed, over the low roofs, a third ball could be seen hanging from the gaff of the signal mast and swinging in the wind.

They fought their way up through the sand, which blew piercingly across their faces. Up at the signal station people were crowded

65

together, women and children, peering over at the bay with their heads bowed.

All the boats were out on the water. The sea was raging, and sea spray lined the long coast. Out by the sandbank, where the waves broke, some of the boats could be seen—two—three—four. They were motorboats being thrown around on the rough sea like nutshells.

"The lifeboat is being pulled out," shouted the people above, but its crew was at sea, only the reserve crew, the old people, were at home. The storm grew and howled through the masts and rigging of the first boats, now happily reaching the land.

"Let's go down," said Nielsen.

The sand was driving into their faces like snow, so that the two men had to turn their backs to the wind while walking down to reach the beach. There were now four of the boats ashore, while five others had reached the nearest sandbank, from where they had an easier job. The engines hissed and rattled, the boats turned leeward and ran alongside the troughs, then turned sharply and swept over the waves into calmer waters.

One boat after another came in, and all hands took hold to drag them onto the beach. Everyone helped, women, children, even the tourists.

After all the motorized vessels were saved, the smacks began to show up behind the sandbanks. They flew around with their flapping sails like pieces of cork, but gradually came closer and closer, eventually they crossed the last bank and came ashore.

And now they were all there—all, with the exception of Jens Laursen's "Betty."

"All but Jens Laursen," traveled the word from mouth to mouth. His boat was not even in sight.

"Let's go up the hill again," said Nielsen. "The boat that's missing is just our boat. It was undoubtedly far out past the great sandbank and therefore could not reach it as quickly as the others. Silius Petersen says his son was in sight just before the storm broke out; they saw him driving out into the open sea."

"Maybe they're going the same way as Lars Jensen's team to Norway last year? What do you think, Silius?" the doctor asked.

The old man shook his head. "In this weather? No, Jens Laursen is certainly more than daring, but that he would not dare . . . Isn't there a boat coming?"

It was not a boat. The rain mingled with the foam of the waves and fell belting down on the mountains of water.

Nielsen and the doctor climbed back up to the lookout while the lifeboat was pulled slowly over the beach below. Upstairs they met Mrs. Weston.

"Is it dangerous?" she asked.

Nielsen looked at her seriously, "It's always dangerous to land on this coast in such weather. And the boat is not in sight yet. But we can hope."

"Will the lifeboat go out?" her voice was calm and composed.

The doctor came up, "I heard it's not going out until there's really something for the rescue team to do. And if that is long in coming, the lifeboat can't set out at all."

"Why not?" she asked.

"Because the sea is getting higher and higher, so the lifeboat itself might find it hard to stay afloat beyond the second sandbar."

Mrs. Weston didn't reply.

"What a mishap," said the doctor, "that Mr. Weston and Mr. Throgmorton had to choose this very day!"

"But initially Mr. Nielsen also wanted to go out," said Mrs. Weston as she pulled her loden coat closer and wrapped her scarf around her neck once more. Nielsen looked at her. The scarf was familiar to him; it had the same pattern as the one he found in the cellar.

"Are you afraid?" he asked her.

She smiled, "Fear? Why? I'm on dry land."

"I mean, for the two men out at sea."

Her face darkened. She didn't reply.

"Let us go back down," said the doctor. "I see they're all pointing to the sandbank. Of course, I can't see anything out there, but the fishermen have better eyes than we do."

A crowd had gathered around the lifeboat. The tourists sought shelter from the wind and rain behind the large red-painted vessel and spoke in muted, solemn voices to the fishermen above who, wrapped in their stiff oilskins, had already taken their places, while old Larsen, the captain, looked out over the sea with a long telescope.

"The two Englishmen are out there too," the crowd whispered, and all eyes were on Mrs. Weston as she approached, accompanied by

Nielsen and Koldby.

The local doctor, Dr. Madsen, who had treated her sprain, stepped up to her and bowed to his patient. He was a pleasant man and spoke English quite well.

"Jens Laursen is one of the village's most experienced fishermen," he said. "He has experienced worse than this. There's no reason to worry."

"I'm not worried," replied Mrs. Weston.

Nielsen looked at her carefully. No, she was not worried—no more than if the two men had been complete strangers to her.

"Doctor," said Madsen whispering to Koldby, "these English women are very strange creatures. There she stands now, straight-faced, cold-hearted—now she even smiles at your friend; they have nerves of steel, these ladies from that smoke-covered island nation."

Koldby shrugged, "Maybe it doesn't matter to her what's happening out there."

"What? Her husband and her brother?"

"Of course. Why not?"

"Are you really not worried?—" Nielsen asked, catching the doctor's last words, "—Mrs. Weston."

She looked at him sharply. "What is the use of that?" she replied, and Nielsen noticed that she almost smiled at the words.

"See the two women there," he said seriously. "They are the wives of Niels Hansen and Jens Petersen. All their hopes are out on the water, and they're staring at the sea all the time."

"I do that, too," interrupted Mrs. Weston. "But what in the world is the use of that? I wish they'd let the lifeboat set out to sea, it's of no use here."

At that moment there was a murmur among the crowd, and everyone pointed excitedly to the sea.

"The boat is in sight," said Nielsen shortly.

It really was in sight. The crowd parted, and the lifeboat was pushed into the water. It floated, and the men in their heavy oil-jackets swung themselves over the side of the ship to their seats, while old Larsen took the helm. The boat, once lifted by the waves, flew up, then the men laid out the oars—there was a creaking sound through the wood and a ringing through the metal plugs—then the boat shot forward into the waves.

The people standing on the shore watched with eager eyes, as the long red vessel was now half-turned broadside, as if it wanted to find a diagonal path through the waves.

And now the "Betty" was in full view—outside behind the last shoal. But the falling rain grew stronger, blurring everything with its streaks of gray, through which appeared, like two swaying shadows, the "Betty" chased by the wind and the lifeboat that had now changed course and headed toward it.

They could see that the "Betty" was pulling down her main sail, and old Silius shook his head.

"What's going on?" Koldby asked, and Silius said, "They'll see. Jens Laursen will not accept the lifeboat; he wants to try to reach the land without help. That would be the way of young daredevils, and the two Englishmen, I mean, can hardly hold him back. These English are tough customers."

The lifeboat had, meanwhile, approached the third sandbank, but the "Betty" ignored it, she lifted her white hull out of the waves, and then slipped into some quieter water.

"He has succeeded," said Silius, "but the hardest is yet to come."

"He's crazy for trying to land in such weather," chided the doctor, "why the hell doesn't he take the lifeboat?"

"He has a good catch on board," said Silius, "which is lost when he leaves the boat. His vessel is insured, but the catch is not. If he leaves the boat to its fate, and it is driven ashore somewhere north of here, and the catch is then washed overboard . . . Judging from what the others have caught, his lobster load is worth about a hundred kroner, and Jens certainly doesn't want to lose that."

The fisherman's wife came up to Silius.

"Do you think Jens will switch to the lifeboat?" she asked.

"That would not be like him," replied the old man.

"God be merciful to him then," she whispered.

"Jens has done well so far. But one should not challenge Providence."

The woman wiped her eyes with her hand. "It was just such a storm back when Jens Molle was lost," she said in a low voice.

"That's right," he replied calmly.

"But now they seem to have some sense," the doctor said. "They took a line over from the lifeboat."

The two boats swayed in the waves, which didn't rise that high between the shoals. On the "Betty" the sails were brought down, so that now the bald mast swung in a wide arc from side to side. Then the fishing boat was pulled to the side of the lifeboat. At that moment the waves were so high that they hid the two boats from those standing on the shore, but when the waves had fallen again, they saw that the two boats had separated again. The lifeboat turned in a wide arc toward the land, while the "Betty" stayed behind.

"Almighty!" cried the fisherman's wife, "Jens is setting his sails again!"

She was right. Betty's sails had been raised again—Jens had chosen to challenge Providence after all.

"Your friends are probably in the lifeboat," said Nielsen to Mrs. Weston.

"No doubt," she replied, her face showing no movement.

The two boats were already several yards apart, the lifeboat shot toward the land, while the "Betty" danced on the waves and tried to catch the wind.

Suddenly there was a shrill cry from the throats of all those who stood on the beach. The "Betty," which was lifted up by the waves at the sandbank and stood in a veritable barrage of breakers, was at that moment caught by a counter-wave on the other side, and whirled around, causing her green-painted keel to be visible over the dark water.

It was a single long cry that sounded on the beach. The lifeboat turned back and headed for the waves again. And when the rain had driven the foam away, two people could be seen sitting on the keel of the capsized craft, fighting for their lives and holding onto the sinking boat. Like a shark, the red lifeboat shot toward them, cleaving the water.

"It will work," said Silius, "they will reach them in time."

The lifeboat slid beside the capsized vessel and lay beside it for a few minutes.

"Why don't they turn back to the coast?" asked the doctor, after a few minutes of keen attention had passed without the lifeboat approaching the shore.

"I don't know," said Silius softly—Then a whisper went from mouth to mouth.

"There were five people on the boat," said Silius. "Niels Hansen's son, the two Englishmen, and also Niels and Jens. One or two of them must still be out there, maybe even three. May God have mercy on them. The current must have already driven them who knows how far north. They are lost."

The minutes dragged along like hours, while the big red boat was lifted over the shoals and finally hit the beach with a loud crunch and crash.

Niels Hansen's wife knelt on the sand, and the crowd gathered around the boat full of urgent questions. Nielsen followed closely behind Mrs. Weston; she had not said a word, but she saw what had happened.

The men climbed out of the vessel, including the tall Englishman who swung himself over the side bench. He nonchalantly scanned the crowd and then sauntered toward Mrs. Weston.

"It's John," was all he said.

Nielsen saw her chest rise and fall. Then, without saying a word, she turned aside and walked up the beach beside Weston.

But among the crowd a rumor spread, "One of the Englishmen is still out there."

Chapter Six

There was a strange, solemn silence over the hotel when the guests gathered for dinner. They had talked about the drowned Englishman, had said everything that could be said—and they had forgotten and forgiven him everything—for the sake of the courage he had shown. Whatever one might say about him, he had been a brave lad. *De mortuis nihil nisi bonum.*

And now he lay out there, a plaything of the wind and the waves; perhaps the sea had taken him forever, at best the waves would wash him ashore far to the north.

And the ladies shuddered at the thought.

Mrs. Weston had not come to the dinner table. But Mr. Weston, as usual, took his place next to Nielsen. His voice was muffled, as it should be, but he didn't seem to be worried. This all made perfect sense to Nielsen. He already gathered that the bond that had held these two men together had not been friendship. Nielsen was convinced that Throgmorton had been the leader in all undertakings, and he had no doubt that Weston's work would be greatly facilitated by his death. As long as Throgmorton, the more ruthless of the two, had been alive, Nielsen had to be careful. But, as Throgmorton now rested in his over-damp grave, Nielsen hoped he might be spared any further trouble.

Weston told him the whole story. The storm had surprised them as they crossed the big bank. It had come, heavy and sudden, as it often happens in the Skagerrack, and Jens had turned for home. Even though the sea was getting higher and higher, the boat kept its course, and Weston didn't think that they were in danger. When they saw the signal on the mountain, the skipper asked them if they would board the lifeboat, but Throgmorton told him that they would follow Laursen's wishes. So, they decided to try landing without the lifeboat. There were about two hundred pounds of lobsters in the ship's hold, and Jens was reluctant to let them go. However, when he neared the third shoal, he began to have doubts, and he signaled the lifeboat to catch up. Weston and Niels Hansen's son, whose life Jens Laursen didn't want to endanger, got into the lifeboat while the others stayed behind;

72

Throgmorton also didn't want to leave the sailor, and they let him have his way.

Finally, when the Betty capsized, Throgmorton was probably caught in a rope or rigging and dragged under the boat.

The vessel itself drifted north, bottom up, so it would probably hit the shore near Lyngby. And Weston wanted to go there that same evening, along with some fishermen, to find the body.

Nielsen offered to accompany him, but the Englishman didn't seem to wish it. "Throgmorton is dead," he said, "and what now has to be done, I can accomplish on my own."

"And Mrs. Weston?" Nielsen asked.

"She has retired to her room," Weston replied. "Her brother's sudden death has badly upset her."

That ended their conversation that evening. The wind weakened considerably toward sunset, so that the tourists enjoyed a rather nice evening. Nielsen and the doctor walked down to the beach and watched the sun go down. The beach was crowded with many people, all of whom walked northward, peering out over the surface of the water, looking for the dead Englishman.

Nielsen and Koldby, too, turned northward, and soon, with the rapid pace they struck up, left all the others far behind.

"Now we've reached the third stage in our affair," said Nielsen, "and I think it's time we got to work. Maybe Mr. and Mrs. Weston will be leaving now and we'll be left without answers."

The doctor nodded in agreement. "Possible. At any rate, Throgmorton was the leader of the trio; we will be able to deal with the other two more easily. They are probably only indirectly involved in the murder, so that Major Johnson, who lies in the cellar, has now been avenged by fate itself. How do you intend to proceed?"

Nielsen thought hard.

"First, I'll tell Weston everything we know. The murderer is dead, and the other two, as we have seen, have also suffered at his hand. The shadow of his crime is still darkening her life. Let us enlighten everything and then set both of them free again."

"That would be too dramatic," said the doctor, stopping.

The sun had now fallen behind the horizon, and all the other visitors on the beach had meanwhile turned to go home; no creature could be seen near them—they had already reached the cliffs of Furreby.

"If we haven't made a mistake yet," said Nielsen, "we will not make one going forward."

The doctor didn't answer, but turned in thought towards the sea, which, after the storm, broke in heavy waves against the cliffs.

Suddenly he grabbed Nielsen by the arm.

"There," he called. "See there!"

Nielsen stared at the sea. At a distance from them, the waves were just driving a body to the land. They hurried to the spot—it was the drowned Englishman. Helpless, wrapped in his long brown loden coat, his face turned down into the sand, his body was slowly lifted to the beach by the waves.

"If you and I were not stubborn freethinkers," said the doctor, "we would now fold our hands and say that the will of God has come. But instead, we find it quite natural, for the corpse to be washed ashore here."

Nielsen stood thoughtfully and indecisively. The doctor, on the other hand, knelt down and turned the body over so that it lay on its back. The face had a calm expression and was not puffy; it was like that of a sleeper; his eyes were half-closed and his beard full of foam. Quickly the doctor opened the coat, and before Nielsen realized what he intended, he had pulled a small brown wallet from an inside pocket of the dead man's coat.

"What are you doing, Doctor?" Nielsen exclaimed involuntarily.

"Checking if his passport is in order," he replied. "He has, after all, just landed." The twilight, which was beginning to fall, was still sufficient for reading, and the doctor eagerly emptied the wallet, which contained several papers in addition to several banknotes.

Nielsen shook his head disapprovingly, "You'd better leave that, Doctor. So far we have avoided any conflict with the police; this is illegal."

The doctor looked up. "Maybe," he replied calmly. "He can keep the money for himself, I just want to look through the papers. To do otherwise would be foolish. It should not be in vain that he has been washed up at our feet." Nielsen shook his head again, but he said nothing. And the doctor unfolded the wad of papers. The loden coat and the tightly buttoned jacket, as well as the leather of the small wallet, had preserved them somewhat. The writing was partly blurred, but not illegible.

Suddenly the doctor jumped to his feet. "Nielsen," he cried, "here are four letters addressed to Throgmorton and another three, which are addressed to Mr. Charles Weston. What on earth did this man have to do with Weston's letters? He can keep the money, but I am keeping these letters. In fact, I will search the whole corpse. Now that we have him where we want him, he's going to open his pockets."

Nielsen looked around involuntarily—they were alone on the beach.

The doctor silently searched the corpse, but found no other papers. Finally, he took the dead man's watch out of the pocket of the loden coat and opened it.

"Nielsen," he said in astonishment, "look here: the inside of the lid is engraved, 'Charles Weston 1885'. Throgmorton carries letters destined for Weston and a watch, which also bears the name of Weston. What does this mean? Yes, if it were Johnson's letters and Johnson's pocket watch, but Weston's . . .? While Mr. Weston, looking for the corpse, now walks all the way along the coast. I mean, by taking these things, I'm doing Mr. Weston no small service, and I even think we can make Weston admit all. I should be very wrong if these objects were not the key to the whole puzzle."

Nielsen unbuttoned his jacket in nervous excitement. "What now?" he asked.

"Well, over in London we've already left a corpse on its own, so here we shall do so again. Just let him lie here and go home. One of the fishermen will soon find the body. And Mr. Weston, I mean, will not report to the police that something is missing as he can only want to be rid of the police as quickly as possible. He already asked me this afternoon what action the authorities would take, and he certainly didn't ask, out of idle curiosity. On the contrary! But now let us turn the corpse over as we found it."

No sooner said than done. Then they walked away as the tide receded farther and farther from the dead man, who lay face down in the sand.

Everything was quiet in the hotel that evening; the piano was silent, the guests sat in small groups, and spoke in whispers. But Nielsen and Koldby were sitting in the latter's room, smoking their cigars and reading the letters they had found.

"We must get them in the right order," said the doctor, "and see how they relate."

75

Four of the letters were business correspondence from Sydney Armstrong.

The first was dated April 25 and contained a brief note on a trivial matter.

The second letter, dated April 28, confirmed the receipt of a letter from Mr. Throgmorton and stated that Mr. Armstrong was ready to get a tenant for the major's house.

The third letter contained a receipt for duties paid and confirmed that the majors' letters, as requested, would be sent to Hjørring to General Delivery. The date was blurred and illegible.

The fourth letter contained the question of whether the house should be rented out after three months, and an indication that the current tenants were willing to rent the house for six months.

The last part of this letter was particularly interesting; it said, "As for Miss Derry, I have to inform you that this lady hasn't come to see me since my telegram of May 4th. It seems that she has calmed down and given up looking for the major. As far as I know, there was nothing in the newspapers about his trip; people seem to believe in the trip to Burma. I hope that the major has received the two letters I sent. The two gentlemen who live in Cranbourne Grove haven't yet sent me any letters for the major; so none seems to have arrived—I also hope that the major received the check I sent the other day. By mid-July, further sums will be sent."

These four letters were addressed to Throgmorton.

The three others, directed to Mr. Weston, were more affected by the seawater. The paper was not that good, and it took a lot of effort to decipher them. Two of them didn't seem worthy of interest; they were dated from last year and were about money matters. The writer, a certain Charles Smith, claimed a sum of one hundred pounds and threatened legal action.

The third letter was very interesting. Of course, much had become illegible, but the rest contained something very important that struck Nielsen and Koldby immediately.

It read:

Sir! Although I don't know you personally, I allow myself to write to you because I feel compelled to do so. You know that some time ago . . . (illegible) to Major Johnson. You know the major and his unfortunate inclination to gamble. Also, his tendency to . . . (illegible) will not be unknown to you. Mrs. Weston is as unknown to me as you are. But a fellow friend told me that you have been a gentleman in any case. I say: Have been! After the events of last fall, I have a right to do so. It is an unusual thing for a young girl, of course, to write to a stranger because of his wife, but . . . (here five lines were illegible) . . . I can't threaten, my father will not help me, as you know. Judging by what happened so far, I must assume that you and . . . (illegible) want to take advantage of it. But I'm ready to ransom James and leave it to you to set the price. I will pay as much as I can. Think of it as business between us, and come with me to Clarendon Road 117, the home of a friend of mine. You are mistaken if you think I'm completely defenseless, I have . . . (illegible)

Ready to negotiate with you, I wait,
A. Derry.

That was an invaluable document; what could not be read could be guessed, it concerned Major Johnson and was addressed to Weston; the writer was Miss Amy Derry—But why was this letter in Throgmorton's possession? Mr. Weston was alive, living with him, and yet Mr. Throgmorton carried Weston's pocket watch and his letters?

"Nielsen," said the doctor, "it dawns on me that we must return to the question of who the murdered man in the cellar is. So far, we have taken as certain that it is the major. But now many circumstances indicate that we were quite mistaken."

Nielsen nodded; his thoughts had gone in the same direction.

The doctor went on, "I think it's *probable* that the drowned person is Throgmorton. But we also used to believe that Throgmorton, his sister, and her husband had murdered Johnson. On the other hand, we find that Throgmorton carried a pocket watch bearing Weston's name and the letters addressed to the latter. And from that we must conclude that *the* Weston we know, who is sitting with us at the table is not the Weston to whom those letters are addressed."

Nielsen interrupted him. "Let's say straight away, Doctor, that this Weston is not Mr. Weston at all, but—Major Johnson."

"Exactly," said the doctor. "And further, we conclude—"

77

Nielsen interrupted him again, "That the man whose corpse we found in the cellar is not the major but Weston."

"Of course," said the doctor. "We have every reason to assume that these people didn't want to live under the names which belong to them. And only out of consideration for their business connections, especially with Mr. Armstrong, have they kept certain names. The names Throgmorton and Weston were and remain necessary, but the name Johnson had to disappear. We may safely assume that one of the gentlemen is Major Johnson, presumably the one called Mr. Weston. As we have noticed, he doesn't even live with Mrs. Weston, as it should be with a married couple. It is clear, then, that the murdered man is either Weston or Throgmorton."

"It can't be Throgmorton, Armstrong saw him."

"Do we know that?" asked the doctor, "and do we know when? What else do we know about Weston and Throgmorton beyond what we have guessed and what this letter from Miss Derry tells us? Is Throgmorton perhaps Weston—is he not Mrs. Weston's brother, but her husband? She was not especially merciful to either man. And then, is the murdered man Throgmorton? Be honest, Nielsen, neither you nor I know. On the other hand, we are already so deeply involved in the affair that we can't let it rest, and I mean if we want to take any official action anywhere, then nowhere would be more convenient than here in Denmark, where we are known and have secure ground under our feet."

"Do you think we should go to the police?" Nielsen asked in astonishment. "Leaving the solution of the mystery that we find too difficult to a Danish court official? That would mean nothing more than putting Mrs. Weston and the major in jail the very moment when we feel certain that these two are innocent, and when the killer, as you said before, has found his own punishment."

"Yes, of course you are right: for Mrs. Weston as well as for the major and Miss Derry, such a step on our part would be quite unpleasant. And it would be unkind for us to cause them such trouble, while for us there is little cost. But, for God's sake, man, what else do you want to do?"

Nielsen smiled. "We'll refrain from contacting the police, anyway. What I intend to do now is to write to Miss Derry and ask her to come here."

The doctor stared at him open-mouthed for a moment. "You know, Nielsen," he said, "I've often noticed one thing about you, that when your foolish ideas have been washed clean by my presence, you suddenly show yourself to be a very smart young man."

In other words, this meant that the doctor applauded the idea, and the next morning a letter went to London with the Hjørring post, written by Nielsen and addressed to Miss A. Derry, which read as follows:

Dear Miss Derry,

For reasons you'll learn later, I searched for Major Johnson and found him here with Mrs. Weston. Things are much more serious than you think, and it would be best if you could come over. It would also be advisable for Mr. Sydney Armstrong to come over here as well. Please tell him from the tenants of the house at Cranbourne Grove 48 that Mr. Throgmorton has drowned in a boat accident in the Skagerrack, and that Mr. Armstrong really can do no better than to get to Løkken quickly. I can't write any more, but I ask you to trust me.

Yours faithfully, Holger Nielsen.

It was a good day's work the two had behind them. And on the same evening the news spread that the body of the drowned Englishman had been found between the Furrebyer Creek and Lyngby.

The county magistrate himself came to inspect the body, as arguments with the English authorities could possibly follow.

Chapter Seven

"Mr. Nielsen," said Weston the next day after lunch, politely greeting Nielsen on his walk along the beach. "You are a legal scholar and you also understand English well. Would you allow me to ask a question? I am urgently compelled to ask it, and in the present circumstances it is also excusable."

"Please," replied Nielsen, "I'm happy to give any information, as far as I am able." But inwardly he thought, "Ah, he's afraid of the police!"

"Do you object to us going to my room where we can talk undisturbed?"

"Not at all," said Nielsen. And so, they went up to Weston's room.

"I am unfortunately a stranger in this country," began Weston, "and unfamiliar with its rules. The fishermen understand nothing of such matters, and the police officer who accompanied me yesterday during the search was evidently just a sub-officer. You, on the other hand, are a Danish lawyer, and I ask you to tell me what actions will now be taken by the authorities."

"Oh, nothing more than an examination of the corpse," said Nielsen, "a most simple business in which the police chief, as the authorized judge, and the district doctor here, confirm the death of Mr. Throgmorton and the cause of death. The crew of the boat will probably also be interrogated to see if anyone is to blame for the accident. Probably no one is to blame—and that will be the end of the matter."

"But what will happen to myself and Mrs. Weston?"

"You will be asked to make a statement regarding Mr. Throgmorton's identity. And there is nothing else; you know him, and Mrs. Weston is his sister, right?"

Nielsen cast a stealthy glance at the Englishman, who seemed quite agitated.

"They will not demand an oath from us or anything like that?" Weston asked in an apparently calm and natural tone, but Nielsen thought he heard his voice quaver a little.

"No, not at all," he assured. "The whole process is just a formality

80

or not even that."

"But what about the inheritance?" the Englishman asked.

"That will be handled in England." Mr. Weston seemed relieved, but Nielsen continued, "After all, you or Mrs. Weston, or both of you, will have to appear before the civil office in Hjørring to address the settlement of the will, that is, you will make a statement about the estate of the deceased. The matter will then be passed on to the presiding British authority by the Danish Foreign Office."

"And will they demand an oath?"

Nielsen smiled—but he suppressed it at once when he saw the Englishman frowning.

"I think you'll have to swear that you and Mrs. Weston have known Mr. Throgmorton for so many years and are able to testify to his identity. I don't know if that will really be necessary, but neither you nor Mrs. Weston would be embarrassed by it."

"Of course not," said the Englishman. "That is not going to happen today?"

"No, certainly not," said Nielsen. "If you'd like more assistance from me, I'm willing to help you both. Of course, I don't practice anymore, but I am still at your service."

"Thank you," said Weston." I'll talk to Mrs. Weston."

Nielsen left him.

Doctor Koldby sat lounging in his beach chair. The weather was warm and quiet now, all the evidence of the storm had disappeared, only Jens Laursen's "Betty" lay on the beach with several holes and a broken mast.

"Doctor," said Nielsen, stepping up to Koldby, "I've just spoken to Weston, and you know, he's worried about the oath he's supposed to take to establish identity. Now he's in a bind."

"Did he say something about the pocket watch?"

"Not a word."

"He doesn't seem to have said anything to the police officer. This brave official has just described to me the discovery of the corpse with all the details, without saying anything about a missing pocket watch— What's Weston doing now?"

"He is having a discussion with his wife, if she is. I have given him to understand that he will get off lightly today, while he will fare worse before the civil office."

"Worse? Why? The two are just lying."

"He maybe; but her, too?"

"Of course, her, too!" shouted the doctor. "What else should she do?"

"But the oath?"

"Oath? Dear Nielsen, you yourself are one of the harshest opponents of the oath. Once you gave a great lecture in the Copenhagen Workers' Association on how wrong it is to force someone to take the oath—and now you stand there and are convinced of the excellence of the oath. Don't misunderstand me; I didn't expect anything else from you, but it's funny, isn't it?"

"I have never denied that in certain cases the oath is required to uncover the truth. I just insist that any compulsion to confess the truth is incompatible with the sound principles of justice."

"Of course," said the doctor, laughing. "The police should have nothing to say, the rogues, however, have all the rights on their side. That is the principle upon which this affair should be based as well. Long live progress and criminology! The crazier the better!"

Nielsen got a bit annoyed, "There can be no doubt that criminals also have their rights. For example, if Mrs. Weston has her reasons for concealing the deceased's name, then she should not be forced to reveal it by the threat of eternal damnation. Criminals, so to speak, have a right to lie. In principle I oppose all oaths, although I recognize that they are at least more modern than thumbscrews and glowing pincers. But they have little to do with the truth. If it really is in the interest of these people to lie and perjure themselves, then they will."

"That's what I mean," cried the doctor, "but allow me to say that you just tried to prove the opposite."

"I just did that to clear my mind," Nielsen said nervously. "I shall likely speak to Mrs. Weston this afternoon; I offered them my services."

The doctor smiled, "Very attentive of you!"

"Oh, I don't want her to get in trouble, of course. On the contrary."

"Do you intend to tell her the little story of Cranbourne Grove now?"

"No, not yet."

"But?"

"Yes, first of all I must, whatever the cost, find out if Mrs. Weston is directly involved in our crime as an accomplice."

"And then?"

"Then—yes, but I'll put it off for now—let her talk about what she wants to talk about and say nothing of what I know. Finally, I'll delay until Miss Amy Derry appears on the battle plain. Then the major's identity is betrayed and Mrs. Weston will be forced to be open with us."

The doctor put his head to one side.

"My dear Cato Junior, wouldn't playing an open game suit you better? Why on earth do you, the advocate of truth and human rights, want to speak with a forked tongue? Live and act according to your pure tenets, honored sir!"

Nielsen got up and looked out on the sparkling water for a moment; then he turned and said, "Oh, ye of little faith! Do you not know that after the creation of man in his imperfection *the lie* was immediately set aside for him to preserve the imperfection? Through the lie, man maintains his original form; the lie hides what is to be revealed; it has played a starring role down through the ages, it has even been the truth itself. We can't ignore the lie; only if we admit it day by day we can gradually get rid of it, but then the world would have come to its end, and the last man would die."

Koldby said nothing about this philosophical excursion.

Chapter Eight

The official examination of the body was carried out in solemn silence. Mr. Throgmorton was dead and nothing could call him back to life. The skipper of the boat was not reprimanded, for the North Sea and its tributaries have their whims and caprices, which no one can foresee, and which have been disastrous for many a mariner.

It was not assumed that the identity of Mr. Throgmorton was to be doubted, since there was no reason for this. The probate of the will was postponed for the time being, however, the police chief with his officers and an interpreter went to Mr. Weston to register the money found with the corpse. It was a considerable sum, so this measure was required of the authorities.

After a quick lunch at the hotel, the officials left, and Mr. Weston was now free to bury his friend.

The police officer, having left 200 kroner for the funeral expenses in Weston's hands, took the remaining sum found with the deceased with him. All in all, the sum found amounted to 1200 Danish kroner.

Mr. Weston, in his utter ignorance, could do nothing but acquiesce in everything with as much grace as he could muster.

But immediately after lunch, he hurried to Nielsen and complained of his penury.

"Look, Mr. Nielsen," he began, "Throgmorton was our financier. That money actually belonged to Mrs. Weston, but of all of us, Throgmorton knew the most about business, so we left all the money matters to him. We now have only a few Danish banknotes besides the money for the funeral. What should we do now?"

"It would be best if you waited a bit and mentioned the matter to the probate court. Then let's see what the magistrate will say. The best way would be to have the will settled in England, for I don't think the officials here can act on their own authority."

Mr. Weston shook his head, "That's a desperate problem for both Mrs. Weston and me. We can't even get home with the money we have."

Nielsen pulled out his wallet. "Mr. Weston," he said, "I am ready to lend you what is necessary. I can understand that you are in an awkward corner, and since I have given you my word to help you . . ."

"That would go too far," interrupted Weston, "I'm a total stranger to you."

"Well, I think you're a gentleman, Mr. Weston, and your word is good enough for me. Just for the sake of form however, I would like to ask for a receipt for the money."

Weston was evidently embarrassed, but since Nielsen was holding his wallet steadily in his hand, he looked up with some hesitation and asked, "Would fifty pounds be too much?"

"*A nice sum!*" Nielsen thought, but he didn't betray himself. "Not at all," he replied. "I understand that you need so much—you have a lady with you. Only, you will have to give me a few days, because I don't have the amount with me."

"Maybe I can do with less . . ."

"No, no, not by any means," Nielsen insisted. "You will not be able to get away with less. I understand it well. However, in order to be ready for any eventualities, I will have to ask you for your permission to represent you before the probate court. I understand that Mrs. Weston, your wife, is the sole heir. The sum will therefore be paid to you or, if you are not legally bound, to her. All that's left for you to do is to get a settlement in England, and that may well happen within a few days."

Nielsen looked at Weston inquiringly. He was not quite satisfied with the outcome, fifty pounds was over 900 kroner, a considerable sum to hand to the Englishman without ever expecting to see it again. If he and the doctor were right in their hypothesis, then Weston would seize the opportunity to disappear as quickly as possible and take up residence elsewhere. Besides, it was important to keep him in Løkken until Miss Derry and Mr. Armstrong had arrived. Of course, if these two hurried on their journey, then Nielsen could induce the Englishman to a sufficiently long stay just by the prospective sum.

Weston seemed to have made a decision. "Mr. Nielsen," he said, "you have offered to do us a great service. I thank you for that, but I must first talk with Mrs. Weston, you understand . . ."

"Of course," said Nielsen, "of course!" And their conversation was over.

***

As Nielsen and Doctor Koldby walked up and down the dunes in the afternoon, they noticed Mrs. Weston approaching them.

"I'd best step away," said the doctor. "No doubt she intends to talk to you. Pursue as many follies as you have done before and come find me later."

With that, he turned and marched toward Nybæk.

Mrs. Weston approached Nielsen and greeted him with a friendly but serious expression.

"Your friend just left . . . did I drive him away?"

"Oh, no, heaven forbid," replied Nielsen, "he only wants to go for a walk to Nybæk, which I don't feel like, because I'm a little tired."

"That's fine," she said. "Shall we sit down?"

They went to Dr. Madsen's beach chairs, which were both empty, and sat down.

"It's really lovely here," remarked Nielsen. "See how calm the sea is, while yesterday . . ." Nielsen paused awkwardly.

But Mrs. Weston didn't seem inclined to discuss the weather.

"I want to talk to you about business matters," she said. "You're a lawyer and have been giving me great assistance over the last few days, greater than you think. Would you be my legal representative now?"

Nielsen bowed his head and she continued, "I say specifically, *my* lawyer. I know you talked to Mr. Weston, he told me about your kind offer, and I thank you for it. However, Mr. Throgmorton's death has put me in a much more difficult position than you can imagine. It may seem strange that I am addressing you in my distress, and you may think that it would be much more natural if I . . . but enough of that. So, you really are willing to be my lawyer?"

"With pleasure, Mrs. Weston. Only I ask you to consider that I am a stranger and that, if I am to be of use, you must trust me fully. Without your trust, I can't exercise my talents in your interests, and I am accustomed to doing everything I do completely. So, I have to ask you for full information about yourself, about the deceased, about Mr. Weston, in short about everything. Have you considered that, Mrs. Weston?"

Mrs. Weston opened her large, dark eyes and looked at Nielsen with a sad smile. "I have considered *everything*," she said.

"Good," he replied, "then I'm ready."

"You must not lend the fifty pounds to Mr. Weston," she said in a somewhat agitated but decided tone. "That could only cause me difficulty, and you, as well. You would never see your money again."

"Ah!" said Nielsen.

She blushed, "That sounds strange, but it's true. Mr. Weston would leave here and never return. He is not a bad person, no, he also has his good sides, many even. But he is a feeble character—an incurable weakling."

"Mr. Weston is really your husband?" Nielsen asked, holding his breath.

"Yes," she said, but she turned her eyes away as Nielsen looked at her.

He didn't believe her, but he didn't let it show and continued, "Good. But before I respond to your amazing request, I would like to know if there is shared property between you and Mr. Weston?"

"No," she said, "everything, including our house, is mine. Mr. Weston can't dispose of it."

"And who is your lawyer in London?" he said involuntarily.

"Mr. Sydney Armstrong—an agent in South Kensington—handles my business."

"Ah," said Nielsen, who was not surprised, "then it is best that we telegraph him that your brother has died."

Mrs. Weston shook her head, "If that were all, then I wouldn't need you, Mr. Nielsen."

"What else would you like me to do?"

"You have to arrange for Mr. Weston to be held here and lend me a small sum—much less than fifty pounds—so I can go home."

"And then?"

"Then you must represent me in front of the local authorities. As soon as I arrive home, I will send you the money and the necessary papers. Do you agree?"

"Of course," said Nielsen. "Only I need to know something about your relationship with the deceased and about the house you spoke of. It would be most natural if you turned immediately to Mr. Armstrong. Since you don't intend to do that, you must have serious reasons, and I must know those reasons."

"Then you don't trust me," she said sorrowfully.

"Oh, of course, but I must be able to justify my position to both the authorities and Mr. Armstrong. Of course, if you have reasons to avoid this gentleman, I want to respect them, but I would like to know them too, because we jurists, that is, the honorable ones among us, form one great brotherhood and don't intrude upon one another."

"Well, if you want to know: I don't trust Mr. Armstrong. He was my brother's business man and he has made serious mistakes—unfortunately nothing but mistakes. And Mr. Armstrong allowed my brother to use him for everything. I don't think he is dishonorable, but I can't trust him. Now you have my reasons."

"But you have family members at home?"

"No," she replied, "my father, who was a doctor in the colonies, is dead, and my mother died during my childhood. I have no relatives, neither in England nor anywhere else."

Nielsen looked at her with pity. Her big dark eyes, moist with tears, were turned on him pleadingly. But then Nielsen remembered Koldby's words—no, he didn't want to be misled, he kept trying to explain how things were.

"You spoke of your house earlier," he said relentlessly, "or didn't I understand you correctly?"

The sun had now sunk completely behind the horizon.

"Shall we walk a little?" she asked with a shiver as if she was feeling cold.

Nielsen rose willingly. At the same moment, the looming apparition of the Englishman appeared at the top of the path to the dunes. Mrs. Weston saw him too.

"Come this way," she said quickly, and they turned to Nybæk. After walking a short distance in silence, Nielsen repeated his question. "You spoke of a house . . ."

"Yes," she replied, "I have a house in London, it's probably rented right now, but it's mine. Mr. Armstrong sees that everything is alright there. He managed it for my—brother."

Nielsen thought she was hesitant about the word brother. It struck him that she rarely spoke of her brother, and when she did, her words sounded cold and sharp.

"Where is the house?" Nielsen asked.

"In South Kensington. But you don't know London, so there's no point in telling you the road."

Of course, Nielsen knew where the house was. She called it her house, Armstrong had called it Major Johnson's house. If she went to London now, she would immediately find out who the tenants of the house were, and then—Nielsen felt—it was all over. His first impulsive decision was to tell her that he was her tenant—but at that moment he saw the doctor approaching them.

"Mr. Nielsen," Mrs. Weston asked hurriedly, "do you have full confidence in your friend?"

"Unconditional."

"And you tell him everything?"

"Usually, yes."

"Will you also tell him what I asked you to do?"

"If you don't mind."

She paused for a moment, "All right, tell him."

Nielsen smiled, "What you've entrusted to me so far, Mrs. Weston, I could tell anyone. We both have eyes to see your relationship with Mr. Weston. And we also noticed that you and your brother were not on friendly terms with each other. Oh, Mrs. Weston, you don't trust me. You only entrusted to me what I already knew. But I will still do what you asked me to do. Tomorrow then."

"And if Dr. Koldby advises you against it?"

"He won't do that. He is a compassionate person and admires you."

The doctor came up to them. "Good evening," he said.

Then they all returned together. Mr. Weston stood in the doorway of the hotel and followed Nielsen with his eyes. Later, he went up to Nielsen and said he hoped Mrs. Weston would agree with him. Nielsen replied that he also hoped so, and that he would write that evening for the money. Then Mr. Weston returned to his room, reassured.

Chapter Nine

"Well, Nielsen," said the doctor late at night, as they smoked their cigars, "have you stood your ground?"

"Almost," answered Nielsen.

"That means you didn't stand it, but retreated while your opponent came out victorious, doesn't it?"

"Perhaps," said Nielsen, who didn't quite want to admit it, "anyway she was cheaper than Mr. Weston. She also warned me against lending money to him. Yes, and it seemed to be her honest opinion. She wants to get rid of him without a doubt, that's clear."

"Well, come out with the whole report," the doctor said shortly, and Nielsen told him what had happened.

"Hmm, hmm," said the doctor, pacing up and down in his room, "you haven't done anything ridiculous, though it's clear that you've been looking pretty deeply into the eyes of this pretty lady. Well, that may be your right—but she has told you nothing but lies, and that is not her right, and you must not be fooled either."

Nielsen said nothing.

"I will set aside her father and her mother, who are dead," continued the doctor. "They're none of our business. *Requiescant in pace!* We know Mr. Armstrong; he is undoubtedly a scoundrel. By the way, I congratulate you on the fact that you haven't revealed your acquaintance with him; it would have been genuinely Danish humor if you had called out: 'Holy Moly! Why, I know that man!' You really have good diplomatic talent, young man. And that you didn't know anything about the house at Cranbourne Grove 48 was also very clever of you. However, you are right: as soon as Mrs. Weston receives the papers from Armstrong, of course she will know about us."

Nielsen interrupted him, "But I still can't understand by what right you accused her of lying!"

The doctor laughed, "Ha! Now Cupid's victim speaks! Put your over-heated feelings for this lady aside for just a moment, and with reason, consider soberly what she has revealed to you. First of all, she claims that Throgmorton is her brother. I very much doubt it. When a brother and sister are on such terms, they don't live together, but separately. I think the so-called Mr. Throgmorton was Mr. Weston. That's the idea I came up with at Nybæk. And the tall Englishman she's about to get rid of is the major. That is clear. So, she lied, like the serpent in Eden, right?"

"You have no right to say that," was Nielsen's answer. "We've made it a rule not to jump to conclusions, and you do so now."

"No, my friend, not at all. You just don't want to see. If the tall man was really Mr. Weston, then they would either be divorced, or they would really live together as husband and wife. Then she would not hand him over to you and run away alone, which is her intention. I don't mean to say that she will not refund your money to you—though ladies may be forgetful in this respect—but you will not see her again. The house really belongs to her; so, she will go straight to Armstrong, the rogue, and—discover that you and I are her tenants. Immediately she will be filled with suspicion, quickly sell everything she has, and disappear into the colonies! She will be gone where we can no longer reach her. In the meantime, Miss Derry will arrive here—of course alone, because Mr. Armstrong is far too clever to be lured here. And then we're sitting with the tall one and Amy No.1. Only the cat is still missing to complete the company."

The doctor sat down after giving this long speech and smoked like a chimney.

Nielsen seemed to enjoy himself. "Dear Doctor," he said, "it's usually not your style to gallop along like this. If Mrs. Weston really had the intentions that you so gallantly grant her, why on earth would she bother to talk to me as she did?"

The doctor laughed sarcastically, "Better say: give you her trust! That's more accurate."

Nielsen thought for a moment. "Do you think she only talked to me just to stop me giving that fool the fifty pounds?"

"Something like that," the doctor looked at Nielsen sideways and laughed good-naturedly. "I'm sorry for you, my boy, but I really think so. You should now reciprocate her confidence and introduce yourself as the tenant of Cranbourne Grove 48, South Kensington, London; explain to her that you are quite satisfied with the house, just not with the cellar under the dining room where we have found a cat! Then, by the way, you remark that Madame Sivertsen has taken over the care of the cat but has no idea of the silent cellar dweller. Mrs. Weston either will not understand what you mean, and may decide to look herself in the cellar, or she'll understand you very well and then probably grow a little faint from fright. You can call me in then if you don't know how to help her—I'm a doctor, after all. Well, what do you say now?"

"Clever little thought, dear Doctor! In the former case, we risked having hell to pay because . . ."

"We can safely leave the former case aside. She certainly knows about the silent cellar dweller. If she is innocent, she has no reason to hide his name. If she is complicit . . ."

Nielsen interrupted him sharply.

"Do you really think *she* could be a murderer?"

"*She*!! Yes, *she*! Right, underlined thickly? Of course, in your eyes she is an angel, just an angel. In mine, on the other hand, she is nothing but something questionable—an X—But you know what? Just accompany her to London! Or rather, suggest that to her. If she really wants your help, then she will accept your offer. If she says no, we know where we are with her. There you have my opinion."

"Why didn't you say that right away, Doctor? That's really clever."

The doctor shrugged, "Only in comedies and bad novels is the right thing said first. In life it is always the other way around. This thought came to me only now as we spoke. But it is really great, isn't it?"

"Excellent," confirmed Nielsen.

"Well, then we will agree again. So, offer the lady your companionship and then look deep into those beautiful eyes. Meanwhile, I'll have the dubious pleasure of keeping a close eye on Mr. Weston. Hang me if that's going to be fun. Still, I will do it conscientiously. But I'd like to know how you're getting down to business—I mean, to our criminal inquiry?"

"As before," said Nielsen shortly. "To confess it openly, I am unable to see clearly myself."

"And I!" snorted the doctor. "But what's your latest theory?"

Nielsen lit a fresh cigarette and, gathering his thoughts, paced up and down.

"Well, speak, Mr. Lawyer," cried the doctor, sitting astride his chair as if it were a horse.

Nielsen hesitated with the answer, "To tell the truth, Doctor, I don't think my hypotheses are worth a lot, but since you want to hear them, just listen: Well, first of all, Mrs. Weston is really Mrs. Weston."

"Because you believe in her steady as a rock," interrupted the doctor.

"Yes! Up to now!" replied Nielsen. "The so-called Mr. Weston is probably Major Johnson. That's what you also suspect. Who, on the other hand, has been murdered, I don't know. I think Mr. Throgmorton, Mrs. Weston's brother. After all, the drowned Englishman is, I believe, Mr. Weston."

"All right," cried the doctor, "but what about Amy No. 1, Miss Derry? Do you suppose that she could really love and long for that tall, gaunt idiot, in spite of all his folly and his delirious infatuation with Mrs. Weston, who, in turn, doesn't care?"

"It may be possible," replied Nielsen.

"What about the cat?" the doctor asked.

"Yes," said Nielsen with a smile, "the collar, which used to adorn Amy No. 1's cat, was transferred to Amy No. 2's cat—the house cat of Cranbourne Grove. Amy No. 1 does not want to do without either the collar or the major; she has already gotten back the former, she will want the latter."

"In other words, we now know the whole story!" laughed the doctor. "Except that it's unclear to us why Throgmorton was murdered and who murdered him. Don't you think it would be more prudent to assume that the major, blinded by his love for Mrs. Weston, killed her husband, and that her villainous brother had used this opportunity to manipulate both of them?"

Nielsen made an impatient gesture, "We had that idea before, my friend. So, we haven't made any progress."

"Perhaps you're right—But now I am going to sleep. Maybe my pillow has some suggestions. That sometimes happens to be the case. So, it is agreed that you should go to London with Mrs. Weston?"

"If she wants me, yes."

"And if she doesn't?"

"Then I'll take a more brutal tack with her."

"You mean, tell her everything you know?"

"Not everything, but enough to show her that we are serious."

The doctor shrugged, "My dear Nielsen, we are constantly going in circles. In the end, *we* will have been the ones who killed the unknown man, and they will bring us in as criminals. Not my preferred

93

outcome."

"Nor mine," said Nielsen, laughing. "Good night!"

And with that they parted.

Chapter Ten

The next morning, Nielsen sent a note to Mrs. Weston asking if she would go for a walk with him. She agreed, and soon afterwards they wandered off to the north.

Mrs. Weston was scared and flustered. She realized that Nielsen intended to talk to her while she wanted to keep quiet. And Nielsen, in turn, noticed how upset she was and decided to be on his guard.

"Mrs. Weston," he said, "I spoke with my friend, and we have both considered carefully what you told me yesterday. I haven't your confidence, which I asked you for; therefore, allow me to ask you a few more questions before we do anything. First, do you wish to divorce Mr. Weston?"

She didn't answer, but she bowed her head affirmatively.

"Good," said Nielsen, "that would be point one. I will not ask for your reasons. My opinion is that every woman has the right to leave her husband if she pleases; and your marriage, as far as I know, has remained childless. So, the thing is simple enough. Does Mr. Weston know about it?"

"No," she replied, "but he will learn of it as soon as it is necessary."

"My next question," Nielsen went on, "is this: Are you completely independent of your spouse in pecuniary matters?"

"Totally," she answered shortly.

"And you are your brother's only heir?"

"As far as I know, yes. But after all, there is nothing to inherit from him." Nielsen pricked up his ears. "My brother has undoubtedly left far more debt than cash, and even more than he possessed, if he possessed anything at all."

"Are you sure about that?" Nielsen asked.

"No, I never tried to get my brother's trust. He was not a good person and . . . but now he's dead."

Nielsen was silent for a moment; then he said, "So it was a kind of deceit by Mr. Weston that he wanted to borrow money by pointing out that you were the heir and that he would inherit through you. I now understand why you warned me and thank you for that. It pains me that an Englishman is capable of acting in such dishonorable manner. Mr. Weston should be careful that such things don't reach the court; he would be facing serious trouble."

Mrs. Weston looked up a little worried. "You didn't quite understand me, Mr. Nielsen. I mean, Mr. Weston is not wrong. He really is entitled to some of the money, because—you understand—he's one of the creditors my brother owed money to."

"Ah!" said Nielsen, but when he noticed that she was quite confused, he continued, sharply, "Do you mean that Mr. Weston has a fortune?"

"Yes," she replied.

"Then why doesn't he write to England and have them send him the necessary funds?"

She hesitated for a moment, then she said, "Mr. Weston has been unwise enough to take part in my deceased brother's businesses—businesses that are not quite, how should I say—not quite worthy of a gentleman. He gave my brother authority, and everything that came to him from England first had to pass through my brother's hands. Now you may understand why Mr. Armstrong, my brother's agent, is not the right man to turn to for legal advice."

Nielsen appreciated her words. "But," he asked, "what about the house?" – *Cranbourne Grove* he had almost said – ". . . the house you mentioned yesterday that you said belonged to you?"

"The house," she replied, "is the only circumstance that compels me to travel to London. It belonged to an aunt of mine; she died the previous year and bequeathed it to both me and my brother. Mr. Weston wished to acquire it, but only Armstrong knows what has become of the purchase. My brother let Armstrong manage it, and it's now leased to two foreign gentlemen. We lived there for only a short time, from there we moved here because . . . because . . . because Mr. Weston wanted to be away from London for a while. The house has caused us much grief and worry; I believe, therefore, that you will spare me the obligation of discussing in detail these things that only torment me."

She looked at him pleadingly.

Nielsen would have liked to learn a little more, and to hear more about the major; but he contented himself with the knowledge that everything she said confirmed his and the doctor's conjectures. Major

Johnson, in possession of funds, had been thrown into the clutches of Throgmorton, while Mrs. Weston was now trying to get away from everything. And what she meant by the grief that the house had caused her, he was able to understand perfectly.

He made a decision.

"Mrs. Weston, "he said," I'm ready to help you, but on one condition: we should go to London together."

"Good, as you wish," she said without hesitation, holding out her hand.

Nielsen was surprised.

She smiled, "I trust you completely. You are the only person in the world that I have faith in, and I will gladly follow you wherever you wish."

There was much in this confession. She also looked at him with a lovely, friendly, and even loving smile.

Nielsen thought he saw behind the dunes the skeptical grinning face of the doctor—he pulled himself together with all his strength, and pledged not to forget the goal he pursued—but Holger Nielsen, the self-proclaimed avenger of justice, the criminalist and philosophical pioneer—he was in love!

He took her hand and kissed it. "Mrs. Weston, "he said in a low voice, "I thank you for your confidence. So we will travel together, and whatever happens, I will do everything I can for you, and show myself worthy of the confidence that I am proud to have won."

She answered with a warm, almost lingering look. Nielsen thought he saw a glimpse of triumph in it—but he didn't see it as Doctor Koldby would have done.

Chapter Eleven

Doctor Koldby gave a long, urgent speech that evening.

"Nielsen," he said, "let me make my diagnosis: you're in love with Mrs. Weston! I've seen it coming for a long time and it's quite normal. You are going to London with her to help her. Fine, I won't say anything about that; I am even inclined to agree with your intentions, because sooner or later you will gain her confidence, and undoubtedly find the solution to the riddle at hand. But this thing also has two sides. Either you really discover everything and then become her accomplice and are complicit in moral and legal terms, at which point, at your request I will immediately discontinue my investigations, which I am more than ready to do at any moment. The man in the cellar interests me only a little. Only you would have to tell me the story, because I'm curious."

"So that would be the first page of your story. And now the second one?"

"The second is the following: Mrs. Weston is pleased to have your companionship because she needs a man to help her out of trouble, for she herself admits she is in a tight spot. She knows she's pretty, the mirror and many gentlemen have told her that often enough, and she has also made a diagnosis: 'He's the right man for my purposes,' she says to herself, adding, 'And I have already caught him!' Yes, because right now you suit her needs. Let us hope that she will be grateful to you for your efforts, but don't be too quickly satisfied, as is common to men in love. Rather, watch out, my boy, don't allow yourself to be carried away by her winsomeness to relinquish the only advantage you have. Promise me therefore—whether your fling now succeeds or not—to refrain from getting fobbed off by her and in no case letting her name be removed from the story associated with this house. I don't want to give a sermon. Act as crazy as you like as far as I'm concerned. And don't let me be prevented from hearing the story of the house on Cranbourne Grove. Take note of that."

Nielsen laughed, "You have no faith in her."

"I don't believe any female being on earth. Let yourself put this lady's collar around your neck—a little necklace with the inscription: Amy's tomcat—*à la bonheur*—there are men who enjoy that sort of thing. The more solid part of the result, on the other hand, I would like to have—full clarity about the story of Amy's cat—all cats of Amy and the cats of all Amys. I won't ask for more. Now give me your instructions before you travel; I will act as *you* wish, for now it has become entirely *your* affair. So, go on, you foolish boy, and meet the fate that awaits you."

"You are a compassionate person, Doctor Koldby. You don't preach, you don't moralize, you are only willing to help. Listen to me: Mr. Weston—let's call him that until we discover his identity—I'll leave him to you. You are responsible for him. Therefore, hold him close. When Miss Derry arrives, she will warn him; whether you release him or not depends on what I discover in London. I have decided to be firm and to assert my will—stop laughing—I have enough willpower. If Amy Weston is as I believe and hope she is, then my true course is at her side."

"And justice comes second," said the doctor.

"Yes, dear Doctor, if love and justice are in conflict, then I will walk on the side of love."

"You've probably read the phrase in a bad novel, my dear Nielsen. But enough of this. I have received my orders. Now go! Onward to your fate and be sure to inform me of the answer to this riddle. Otherwise I'll renounce your friendship, honored friend."

"Just rely on me," Nielsen said soothingly.

"The devil I will! When a man is in love and courting, then there is as little relying on him as on a woman, and every friendship with him is in danger. A classic friendship, as in Cicero and Seneca—in Latin *amicitia*—is only possible between very pure men. But let us part on that sad note and go to bed. Because early tomorrow your escape and the lady's will begin. The coach leaves at half past five. I will seek to keep a good memory of your name in honorable Løkken."

"Fine," said Nielsen, "but above all, pay attention to Weston."

So, they both agreed—or rather all three.

Part 3
Amy's Puss

Chapter One

Løkken, 4 July 19–

Dear friend and comrade!

In keeping with my promise—for I am in the habit of keeping my promises—I will give you a meticulous account of everything that has happened in the respectable town of Løkken since the disappearance of Mrs. Weston and a certain gentleman. It didn't take long for this news to spread; just after you left, that donkey of a cloth merchant from Randers grilled me about the news over breakfast. I pretended to be as surprised as ever and got off lightly. I even agreed to prepare Mr. Weston as gently as possible for the blow this news would be. Now listen to how I did it. I went up to him and told him that you had gone to Hjørring to arrange for the money, and that you had asked me to tell him this, adding that it would be advisable for him to take a trip to the Rubjerg Reef because the probate court officer, along with his entourage, would probably pay him a visit today. He wanted to talk to his wife first, but I made a plausible excuse that it would be better if Mrs. Weston did not hear about his plans, so that she would face the officials quite unknowingly if they arrived during his absence.

(Nota Bene: Mr. Weston is the silliest, most gullible, idiot under the sun!)

So, my proposal was accepted, we drove off, followed by the gaze of all the hotel occupants, who evidently believed that we were hot on the tracks of the fugitives. We had rented a car from the brewer and rattled along the miserable road to the reef. It was a difficult test, this ride to the reef, and I could only overcome it by thinking with satisfaction during the whole drive northward that you were headed in the opposite direction with Amy No. 2 at the same speed. So, we reached the reef without any significant event. My companion was grumpy and silent. We ate our lunch, which we had brought with us, drank an excellent red wine, then lit our cigars, and now I thought the time had come to begin my speech.

"Mr. Weston," I said, "allow me to inform you that your wife, Mrs. Weston, eloped this morning with my friend Nielsen!"

Dear Nielsen, have you ever seen a jack-in-the-box? That's exactly how our Mr. Weston from London behaved after my communication. He jumped a yard in the air.

I asked him to stay calm, for you and Mrs. Weston were by now already over the mountains—at least as far as Aarhus and you would soon be in Esbjerg.

I let him scold me for five minutes as much as he liked, and I must confess that the English language has a rich stock of colorful expressions, which, however, made on such a pure, calm, and innocent nature as mine, only a moderate impression. When he seemed to have exhausted his repertoire, I, too, didn't hold back with my eloquence. I can't repeat word for word what I said, but my speech was something like this:

"Sir," I said, "you seem to have finished. So, I will begin. Needless to say, it is completely useless to follow the fugitives; in Denmark, you will not reach them anyway. Besides, you have no money to pay your hotel bill—you will not get anything from me, and if you try to flee, you will be quickly arrested. So, you may complain about me as much as you want, but you will not benefit from it. Your wife has gone to London to arrange her own affairs. She wished to travel without her escort, and only with reluctance did she accept Nielsen's offer to help her. Nielsen is a man of honor—that means Mrs. Weston is in good hands. She has not been kidnapped.

"Sir," I went on—I really did say 'sir' again—"I declare you to be my prisoner. Until Mrs. Weston comes back, I'll hold you hostage. I will provide for your support, tell lies to other guests, in short, be useful to you in every way, except that you must remain under my supervision. If Nielsen returns in a few days, you'll again be a free man."

Obviously, he didn't quite understand. He roused again, talked a great deal about the great nation to which he belonged, and threatened me with the British consul. I listened attentively to him and replied that I would be pleased to go with him to the British consul.

"You treat me like a criminal," he said.

Hereupon I told him that since prisoners usually belonged to this worthless human class, he would be free to consider himself a criminal. I have had reasons, I said, to assume that he has been sailing under false colors. Therefore, if he preferred the supervision of the authorities to mine, I would gladly give my place to the police.

Evidently the police were not to his liking; he collapsed under the force of my logic and in a weak voice asked by what right I treated him this way.

"My friend and I," I explained to him, "have harbored a certain undefined suspicion against you for some time, because of your shyness toward the authorities and other circumstances. As soon as Mrs. Weston or Mr. Nielsen returns from London, you are free. You will have absolutely nothing to do with the police, and I can assure you that you will be released once Nielsen has finished with Mrs. Weston's affairs. A letter from him will suffice. But until he writes, you are my prisoner."

"Do you at least acknowledge that your actions are unlawful?" he asked, now quite calm.

"If they were against your will, yes. But you'll have to admit that you don't have a penny in your pocket. Your wife assured me that the money left behind by the deceased belongs to her as part of her separate estate. So, there is nothing for you to do but submit."

"The money is mine," he said.

"Prove it to the probate court."

"I will!"

"All right, let's go to Hjørring together," I said—But he didn't want that either.

In short, the end was that—like the great donkey that he is—he gradually became quite tractable, especially when I treated him kindly. He assured me that he was a gentleman, to which I assured him that I was convinced; I told him that I had no trace of suspicion against him but was forced by circumstances to act as I had. Eventually, we became good friends, and I promised to help him out of all difficulties. He doesn't seem to be heartbroken about his wife's escape, though he evidently doesn't believe she will ever return. He just wants to go to London.

That's all. Notice well that I have not mentioned any doubts that he is Mr. Weston; neither did I mention Cranbourne Grove, nor the cat. Do as I do and first check how far you can go without giving away our shared knowledge. And for heaven's sake, watch out for your little heart. To tell the truth—it is from this part of your body that I fear will come your greatest follies.

So be on the alert, young man!

Your friend, Jens Koldby.

P.S. Although I'm not a woman, I've written a postscript. When I was about to send this letter, a telegram arrived for us from London. It contains only three words: "Today left London Amy D." —Therefore the *P.S.:* 'Mr. Weston' from London is in for it now!

Chapter Two

London, 7th July 19–

Dear Doctor!

I have received your letter and hasten to answer it. Our journey was a happy one. Mrs. Weston is a pleasant traveling companion and, I believe, thinks the same of me. I had decided not to put any pressure on her for the time being. Our plan was to go to London and visit Mr. Armstrong together. Mrs. Weston is now staying at the Grosvenor Hotel, Victoria Station, where I will also take lodgings. I notified Madame Sivertsen of my trip to London and wrote to her that she should keep my letters there.

For the time being, I will not let Mrs. Weston out of my sight; for this purpose, I have also taken the travel fund into safekeeping. I have given up definitive plans and am widening our view of the affair. On the other hand, Mrs. Weston and I can hardly avoid a visit to the house on Cranbourne Grove, and then I guess I'll have some explaining to do. I don't doubt that the murdered man was her husband, despite her ingenious story about Throgmorton, which led me astray for a while. There can be no doubt about the major, and our views are the same in this respect. I sent a few words to Miss Derry at the steamer address when we were in Esbjerg. She must have gotten them, you should be able to deduce the import of what I have told her from how she behaves. If she's still infatuated with the major, choose the best course you can, but don't forget that you're responsible for both of them. Once the dam has burst here, you should receive clear instructions from me. I am sure that as soon as tomorrow there will be something certain, but you must expect it will take three days to receive accurate information from me. I won't write until I can see clearly how things are. It would only confuse you if I wrote earlier, and you are a man who can be left to act on his own judgment. This letter doesn't tell you much, but you expected to hear from me so I have written. If you write, address your letter to Cranbourne Grove; only telegrams are better sent to the hotel.

Yours sincerely, Holger Nielsen.

Chapter Three

Løkken, 6 July 19–

Dear friend and counterpart!

This letter is an important document. So . . . Amy No. 1 arrived here. Heaven bless the lovely child for this act. She came alone. I did not dare to leave my prisoner unattended, even though he seemed to accept the inevitable. The probate court hasn't yet filed anything, but this will undoubtedly happen soon, as a series of meetings take place tomorrow. But this is incidental, now comes the main thing. After we—Mr. Weston and I—had taken our lunch, I called him up to my room where Miss Derry, ready to receive him, was waiting. He entered —and was identified as *Mr. Weston*! I'll tell you this at the beginning, because this is a letter and not an exciting novel. You and I had wagered our boots that he was Major Johnson—yet he's Mr. Weston. And Amy No. 2 is really his wife.

I don't think I can put a particularly witty face on this, and I refrain from trying to give you a detailed account of the incident.

You won't believe it. Miss Derry arrived, as is right and proper, by car from Vraa; having arrived at the hotel, she asked—also, as it should be—for me. I received her and led her to my room, and she told me that she had received your letter and that she saw that her arrival was necessary. She had also visited Mr. Armstrong, who informed her that he had received a telegram from Mrs. Weston, in which she reported her arrival in London, and that he was, therefore, obliged to wait for her in London. She, Miss Derry, had now come alone to Hjørring, wishing only to know why her presence was necessary. I replied that she would soon see. I brought in Mr. Weston, expecting to see him exposed as Major Johnson. When he entered, Miss Derry stood up calmly and put out her hand toward him with an indeed friendly, and quite natural and even casual *"How do you do, Mr. Weston!"*

That is indeed everything I have to report.

Mr. Weston seemed more emotional than usual, and he and Amy agreed at once that they had something to discuss. I no longer feel secure about my position because, in fact, my role is played out. Miss

Derry thanked me for my efforts and made it clear to me that she no longer needed me. Mr. Weston treated me with too much courtesy. He slips out of my hands. And, yet, what can I do? Sitting still and looking like a fool doesn't suit me. It is clear that our solution of the riddle was murderously wrong!

I think we have to turn our thoughts anew to the man in the cellar. But I can no longer accept hypotheses; I'm heartily sick of it!

That's enough for today. Send me instructions.

Yours, Jens Koldby.

Telegram.
London, 8 July 19–
Doctor Jens Koldby—Løkken.

Weston aka Johnson has to be detained, if necessary with the help of police. Miss Derry should be held along with him.

Nielsen.

Chapter Four

Mr. Armstrong was quite excited when Nielsen and Mrs. Weston paid him a visit. Nielsen had Mrs. Weston do the talking; he had not yet told her about his acquaintance with the agent and greeted him politely like a stranger.

Likewise, Armstrong made no comment about knowing Nielsen, as natural as that would be. He was evidently determined to exercise caution and guard his tongue more than was his custom.

Mrs. Weston said, "This gentleman here is a friend I met in Denmark—Mr. Nielsen. He promised to help me with his advice regarding my inheritance. As I informed you by my telegram, my brother lost his life as a result of an accident, and since, as you know, he had power of attorney, we are now in a troubled position. This gentleman knows Mr. Weston and knows that I have a special property that I wish to have independently. We therefore ask you, Mr. Armstrong, to explain to us how things are. Speak freely, as if only I were present."

Mr. Armstrong bowed.

"If I understand correctly, this gentleman is a lawyer and well acquainted with your affairs?"

Mrs. Weston answered in a clear voice, lingering at each of her words, "Mr. Nielsen knows Mr. Weston and me from Denmark—only from Denmark. He also knew my brother, but only superficially. What I want from you is nothing but to tell us both about my brother's business situation."

Mr. Armstrong gave Nielsen a sharp look, then said doubtfully, "It would be better if Mr. Weston were present."

"I don't wish his presence," she replied. "What I ask for is only complete information about my brother's business."

Mr. Armstrong cleared his throat. "As you wish, Mrs. Weston. Let me start with the house. That will be of interest to Mr. Nielsen too, for, as you well know, Mr. Nielsen is the tenant of Cranbourne Grove 48."

Mrs. Weston looked up in surprise. "Mr. Nielsen?"

He nodded.

"I'm the tenant of a cottage at Cranbourne Grove 48, me and the doctor you know. If the house you talked to me about is in South Kensington, Cranbourne Grove 48, then, yes, I'm your tenant, Mrs. Weston."

Mrs. Weston blushed and said after a moment's hesitation, "That surprises me."

Mr. Armstrong began to feel secure ground underfoot.

"Mr. Nielsen is by no means surprised," he burst out eagerly." When he rented the house from me, I told him it belonged to Mr. Weston."

"Excuse me, sir," cried Nielsen, "you told me that it belonged to a Major Johnson. You said the major bought it from a Mr. Throgmorton. If you mentioned a Mr. Weston, it was only incidentally, as you will well remember."

The agent looked at Nielsen sharply.

"And do *you* perhaps remember," he replied, "that you had questioned me sharply about this very matter, at the behest of a young lady named Miss Derry? And do you perhaps remember that I gave you the address of Major Johnson and told you that the major was probably living with Mr. Throgmorton? Perhaps you also remember writing a letter to Miss Derry and asking her to come to Denmark with me—on the occasion of the death of Mr. Throgmorton? Anyway, you must admit that I have every reason to be surprised to see you here as Mrs. Weston's legal representative, while Mrs. Weston should know that, as her brother's business agent, I have a claim to her confidence."

"Are you done, Mr. Armstrong?" Nielsen asked, amused.

"I wish to know what Mrs. Weston has to say to me about this," was the agent's disapproving answer.

Mrs. Weston touched her handkerchief to her lips with an agitated movement, then said, "Stay with it, Mr. Armstrong. Needless to say, Mr. Nielsen didn't speak to me about these things, since he only met my brother, Mr. Weston and myself in Denmark and not Major Johnson. I am glad to hear that Mr. Nielsen has rented my house, and it doesn't surprise me at all that my brother, who could never act straight if his life depended on it, thought it best to have you tell the tenants that the house belonged to Major Johnson. My brother found you an all-too-agreeable agent, Mr. Armstrong, and that is why I tell you bluntly that I don't wish your services any longer."

"Is that going to be a challenge, madam?" said Armstrong, red with anger.

"It expresses my intention, nothing more. You can take it as you like. Mr. Nielsen has my trust—not you."

"Does Mr. Nielsen really have your full confidence?" Armstrong asked doubtfully.

"Yes," was her answer.

"Even after you have learned that Mr. Nielsen, without telling you a word, asked Miss Derry to come to Denmark?"

"I don't know Miss Derry, nor am I interested in this lady . . . You spoke of the house on Cranbourne Grove . . . Would you be so good as to continue with that? You know that Miss Throgmorton, my father's sister, left the house to me alone, but that I gave my brother authority to administer it for me, and that he misused this authority. You are aware of this, correct? You also know that the purchase of the house by Major Johnson came to nothing at the time, but I respected the convention you set up and allowed you to nominally administer the house for my brother so that he would not get in conflict with the law. He is dead now, and I ask you to present your bill."

"You shall have it," said Armstrong. "I'll prepare an itemization immediately. No one can accuse me of any irregularities in my business."

"All the better. So, my brother's creditors can't touch the house?"

"No."

"Good, and my bank shares?"

"Also, untouched, except, of course, for those your brother pledged by forging your signature."

"And who has these papers now?"

"Miss Derry bought them," said Armstrong hurriedly.

"Ah!" Mrs. Weston brought her handkerchief back to her lips. "You and Miss Derry seem to be good friends. Who is Miss Derry, then?"

"Mr. Nielsen introduced her to me, Madame. He must know her better than I do. Your new lawyer will be able to give you full information about the lady."

Nielsen nodded, and Mrs. Weston calmly continued, "Good. Then we don't need to discuss her any further. Please be so good as to send me your bill."

She rose.

"Shall we go, Mr. Nielsen?"

Nielsen also got up and Armstrong followed them to the door. "I want to talk to you, Mr. Nielsen," he said.

"Oh, that depends on Mrs. Weston," Nielsen replied firmly. "I'm her lawyer and I'm only allowed to act according to her wishes. Is it alright with you, Mrs. Weston, if I have a private word with Mr. Armstrong?"

The woman in question looked over at Armstrong with a smile. "I am sure that Mr. Armstrong understands why I have no confidence in him; on the other hand, I don't find the slightest reason for discouraging others from honoring Mr. Armstrong with their confidence. Act as you please, Mr. Nielsen. I mean, we should talk about what we've just heard, and if you don't mind, let's go to the house in Cranbourne Grove. Since the house is mine and you are renting it, we are both at home there."

Nielsen kept the door open. "I may visit you this afternoon, Mr. Armstrong," he said as he walked.

"Oh, please," Armstrong replied with hypocritical courtesy, "don't make any effort for me." He seemed determined to play the superior again in the end. But Nielsen and Mrs. Weston put an end to his remarks by leaving the room without saying another word.

Chapter Five

Madame Sivertsen was not easily disturbed. Her fat, peaceful countenance usually showed no expression—but when she now opened the garden gate with an honest, friendly smile to Nielsen and saw beside him the strange, elegant lady, she recoiled in astonishment.

Nielsen had to smile and immediately explained. "This is my landlady," he said.

"Ah," drawled Madame Sivertsen, falling back into her old apathy, "the lady who owns the house?"

"Exactly."

As Madame Sivertsen stepped aside to clear the way for them, an unexpected character entered, stage right. With a haughty demeanor expressing pride of ownership and tail held stiffly at forty-five degrees, the cat slowly stepped down the paved garden path.

On Madame Sivertsen's face the broad smile reappeared. "Yes, Mr. Nielsen, Puss has meanwhile recovered excellently," she said. Then she turned to the lady to say good-naturedly in English, "You know, Madame, that this cat actually belongs to you? The gentlemen always called her Amy's Puss. She crawled out of the wall of the kitchen half-starved but now she has gotten so fat and round she can hardly fit through the door, haven't you Puss?"

Puss purred.

"Puss really owes me life and freedom," said Nielsen. "I must tell you that I have freed the cat from the cellar under the dining room, where she was trapped and made herself noticed at night by her miserable meowing."

He spoke in a determined tone, watching Mrs. Weston closely.

She went deathly pale and began to shake violently.

"Shall we go in?" Nielsen demanded while the cat softly snuggled against the lady's dress.

"Mr. Nielsen," she replied, stammering, "I—I'm not well. I think I would do well to take a cab and drive to the hotel. I'm not well."

Madame Sivertsen gave her a long look. Nielsen, however, laid his hand lightly on her arm and said in a whisper, "I insist that you come in

113

with me. Listen, I insist."

A wave of blood rose in her face, then she turned pale again and let Nielsen almost forcefully lead her through the front door. He opened the door to the drawing room, almost mechanically, she entered and sat down in an armchair by the empty fireplace. Nielsen stopped in front of her.

Then she hid her face in her hands and began to cry.

Nielsen was silent.

Finally, she looked up despite her tears, turned her pleading eyes full of despair on him, sobbing and said, "So *that* was it . . . You have hounded me like a wild animal—you, Mr. Nielsen, whom I trusted— the only one in the world I trusted!"

Nielsen was violently moved by her words, he felt his heart drawn to her, but the doctor's sharp-featured, sarcastic smile appeared in his memory like a vision. Had the moment of decision arrived? Did her words confess her complicity?

"Mrs. Weston," he said, "I don't understand you. I certainly didn't hound you like a wild animal. I am ready to help and assist you—now as before. But I demand one thing of you—the truth!"

She didn't answer, but cried to herself, her whole body shaking.

"Mrs. Weston," repeated Nielsen, "be open with me; whatever happened, I will not leave you. I only ask for the truth."

She looked up. "Later," she said, "later. Now I can't, let me go home, let me rest. I am only a woman, this is too much for me. If you want to kill me, do it—but don't stand there and don't look at me so sternly. I swear I'm innocent—really innocent."

Despite Dr. Koldby's sarcastic smile which now, in his imagination, seemed likely to break into open laughter, Nielsen took her hand and stared into her eyes with a look that was much, much warmer, than Dr. Koldby would have found suitable under the circumstances.

Then she straightened up and wrapped her arms around him, "Oh, help me—help me—take me away from this place. I . . . I love you, yes, I always want to be with you . . . always be yours. I love you."

And Nielsen felt her cheek, still wet with tears, pressed against his; then he took her in his arms and kissed her tears away—Somewhere, deep in the recesses of Nielsen's imagination, Dr. Koldby laughed.

* * *

Madame Sivertsen was very displeased that day—and she became even more so when Nielsen asked her to prepare Doctor Koldby's room for the strange lady. She had been hired to run the household for two *gentlemen*!

But she was an experienced person and knew how to follow orders. And Nielsen didn't seem in the mood to tolerate contradiction.

So, she made the room ready, but when dusk fell and she retired to her own room, she pulled Pussy on her lap and said to her, "You see, Pussy, now we've got a lady visiting. Now our good days are over! Oh, how true is it that we ladies are the cause of all the troubles and labors of the world."

Pussy was also a lady.

Chapter Six

Cranbourne Grove 48, 15 July 19–

Dear Doctor!

I wish you were here! There is much to tell you. I must start with this explanation to help you understand how things are here: I have met my fate and, as you colorfully put it, I am Amy's tomcat. I love Amy and Amy loves me. The former two facts you already knew, for the latter you will have to take my word. You have always been intellectually superior to me, both cool and shrewd. I am, therefore, sending you a report of my interrogation of the defendant, Amy Weston. Consider it carefully and advise me if you agree with the conclusion I have reached as examining magistrate. Before doing so, I would like to give you an overview of the case, with all its details, and ask you to keep this in mind as you examine the evidence. It has been a very complicated case, and its separate parts have led us to many joint consultations; it is only these last steps I have been forced by circumstance to take alone. I completed the investigation, and the case approaches its legal conclusion.

The case has two sides: a theoretical one and a practical one. It's based on one fact: On May 4, we both found the body of an adult male in the cellar of Cranbourne Grove 48. The face was unrecognizable, and few if any signs indicating the identity of the dead were present. On the other hand, there was no doubt that a crime had been committed here, that is, an act that would have caused the state authorities to intervene and punish the perpetrators.

The theoretical side is as follows: Was it our duty to summon the state authorities, in this case the London police, and to hand the matter over to them?

We debated the question and concluded that the matter did not concern us and that we had the right to ignore it.

At the same time, however, we agreed that as members of the human race, "any man's death diminished us" therefore, we had an interest in the matter. Thus, this was an opportunity to follow the case from a purely human point of view, and to decide, by our investigation,

116

whether the usual conception of crime should be applied here. This also enabled us to spare those who would have been inconvenienced in the normal pursuit of the cause; we were able to exclude the public, which always causes damage in such cases, and we could follow the straight path without having to follow the many side roads that the authorities must take into account.

We have achieved our purpose because, as you can see from the attached documents, the case is now completely resolved. Whether the act was a crime or not, may be a matter of taste. What you have to decide is whether we should get the authorities to intervene or whether we should handle the case without a court of law.

The practical side of the matter is different: we found the murdered man, we found the cat that told us that it belonged to a certain Amy, and we found two Amys: Major Johnson's Amy and my Amy. Then we set out after the trio: Weston, Throgmorton, and Johnson, while leaving Miss Derry and Mr. Armstrong behind. We followed the trio and found the second Amy. Then higher powers intervened and blew up a storm in the North Sea that removed Throgmorton from the board. At that time, we considered Major Johnson the murder victim, and the other two the perpetrators. This was an error because it was not long before we came to believe that the man who called himself Weston must be the major. And he really is the major, while Mr. Weston is the dead man lying in our cellar covered with lime. Finally, you will see the name of the offender from the enclosed document.

In a few short weeks, we have thus solved the crime—to use the technical expression—with complete certainty. In view of the circumstances, this is quite a respectable achievement.

If we compare our theoretical experience with our practical one, we find that the method chosen by us, from the practical point of view, is excellent. Theoretically, however, it is less satisfying in that the practical resolution of the crime does not help us address the larger question. All of the issues with which we were originally concerned are still mostly present. Mistakes and injustices at the expense of the innocent have certainly been avoided, but the main question remains unanswered, and I will try to dress it in such a form that you can give your opinion on it. The question reads as follows: "Is there any compelling reason for us to present the case to the legal authority and to face its verdict?"

I put the question quite clearly so that you can only answer yes or no.

And in connection with this, I must make a confession. In the course of our research and the subsequent events, I—in the legal sense—became incapable of doing my duty without fear or favor. Theoretically, this means a defeat for us, for it proves that the individual, because of his inherited tendencies, and indeed, because of human nature, is incapable of representing the interests of society. This is nothing new in itself, I just want to draw your attention to it. As far as I can see, it is one of the unresolved problems of existence, how the interests of the individual—of the ego—are to be reconciled with those of society—of the other; I don't hesitate, however, to agree with the famous philosopher Leibniz that one can bring about a resolution of this paradox by giving the individual ego the leading role in every action. In any case, by giving this question to you for decision, while my judgment is compromised, I prove that I have a sincere desire to look at our matter objectively. After this introduction, I leave to you the study of the documents which I have written in accordance with what I have observed and been told, so that you will be able to judge the matter quite impartially. Witnesses were unfortunately not present at the interrogation, as I could not call in Madame Sivertsen, and Amy's cat is would not take the oath, although she played an important role in the affair.

I await your answer and remain

Your sincerely, Holger Nielsen.

***

Original of the interrogation held on July 12, 19– in London, South Kensington, Cranbourne Grove 48, regarding the unknown male corpse found in the cellar of the house on May 4.

The tribunal met at half past seven in the evening and consisted of Holger Nielsen as a self-appointed judge without witnesses. Appearing, free from compulsion and influence, Amy Weston, who stated that she was born on March 1, 18– in Trinidad as the daughter of the late Doctor Charles Throgmorton and his also deceased wife Cecilie Jones. The parents died when the witness was still a child, and she was educated by an aunt in Trinidad. At the age of seventeen she came to London and was taken to the house belonging to her father's sister,

Miss Jenny Throgmorton, who owned the aforementioned house at Cranbourne Grove 48. Amy and her brother John McGregor Throgmorton, elder by three years, were the only children. The brother, who attended the technical school in South Kensington, received, after completion of his studies, employment as an engineer with the Great Western railway company. The witness describes him as a hypocritical, dissolute man who constantly caused her and her aunt sorrow. Eventually he was dismissed from his position and opened an electrician's shop in Lambeth, in company with a certain James Weston, a schoolmate of his. Weston, described by the witness as an active and energetic man, was a frequent guest at her aunt's house and seemed to be a good influence on Throgmorton. The witness's aunt was generally regarded as wealthy, and often made it clear that she intended to leave her entire fortune to her niece. This circumstance was probably what prompted Mr. Weston to pay special attention to the witness. She was twenty-two at the time, and since her aunt was very withdrawn, she had had little opportunity to meet with people and judge them. As a result, when Weston wooed her after knowing her for about six months, she accepted his courting. Not because she loved him, but because she was attracted to him and wanted to change her life.

Responding to the judge's question as to whether she had ever felt love for a man, she resolutely denied, adding that the judge was the first and only man she truly loved, and that this love would last to the end of her life.

The record here reflects a brief adjournment to allow the witness to consult with her lawyer.

Continuation of the interrogation at half past eight.

When asked by the judge, the witness stated that the first years of her marriage could be called "happy" in the ordinary sense of the word. Her husband showed her all possible attention, her brother behaved well, and the business of the two brothers-in-law flourished. But then they were hit hard: they had miscalculated the costs when taking over a public work and were now suffering such heavy losses that they were forced to cease their activities. They were successful in avoiding bankruptcy, but from then on, they struggled with great financial difficulties and often hinted at the desirability of the aunt's untimely death. They plunged into unsustainable speculations of all kinds, which quickly brought them gain, then loss, and Weston's behavior became as debauched as Throgmorton's. The relationship between him and his wife became quite cool, and frequent scenes between them made the witness fearful of more serious friction.

It finally ended with the witness leaving the house in the fall of 19– and moving in with her aunt who was seriously ill and in need of care. At about the same time, Weston and Throgmorton made the acquaintance of Major James Johnson of the 17th Lancers Regiment, who had come to London on a special assignment. The major was still a young, well-off man and betrothed to a young lady, Miss Derry, the daughter of a great businessman; he endeavored to increase his income, since this was always greatly diminished by his inclination to gamble. Through their work with an agent, Mr. Sydney Armstrong, this newly created syndicate Weston-Throgmorton-Johnson was now involved in a building speculation that ended in scandal; the three speculators had considerably exceeded the limits of legitimacy and caused heavy financial losses to many people, especially those on a low income.

Major Johnson was immediately dismissed from the army; Weston and Throgmorton were subjected to an interrogation, which, however, led nowhere, as they could not be held liable. The witness knew that this incident caused Miss Derry's parents to inform the major that they wanted him to cancel his engagement to their daughter. But Miss Derry, as the witness knows, still felt warm affection for the major, which the witness finds all the more inexplicable, as she herself has always felt only aversion to this man. Weston and Throgmorton didn't take long to squander the money they had earned unlawfully on the building fraud, and when the witness's aunt died, soon after, Weston approached the witness, begged her forgiveness, named himself a changed man, and treated her with so much kindness that she agreed to live with him in the house, Cranbourne Grove 48, which she had just inherited.

But she soon came to regret that choice. Major Johnson was now a permanent guest in the house. Quite apart from the distaste she felt for him, she was even less willing to endure his presence when she realized that he sought to impose his companionship on her, a married woman, in the most unseemly and dishonest manner possible.

When asked by the judge, the witness declares that she has never had any feelings other than those described for the major, and that she has always both rejected and repudiated him despite his long, continuous advances.

This explanation prompted another brief "adjournment" of the interrogation, which, however, was soon resumed on account of the importance of the matter.

The witness then reported that Weston surrendered himself to alcohol and waste, while the major, who, in contrast to the other two, lived an outwardly respectable life, became their constant guest. Then, one day, she told the major that she had the impression that the two men were seeking to deceive him for his money; she begged him to remove himself from the house and to leave her in peace. The major didn't seem to believe what she said, and informed Mr. Weston of the situation, calling forth a scene that the examining magistrate, because of its importance, wants to reproduce with the witness's own words (which he has recorded, stenographically).

"I remember that terrible evening—it was April 26—a cold, wet day. About eight o'clock in the evening I had turned on the light and sat here in this room, where we are now, at that table by the fireplace, where you are now sitting. Major Johnson was sitting in front of me chatting and had—I remember exactly—his cat in his lap, the same cat you call Amy's Puss. Then he pulled out of his pocket a small silver chain and told me that it actually belonged to his first fiancée, Miss Derry, whose first name is also Amy. He tied the chain around the cat's neck, as he said, to show me that all his thoughts were only for me. We were all alone at home, because the maid had ceased her employment and the new one would come only the next day.

Then the door was pushed open and Weston, drunk and loudly brawling, came in—even though my brother, who was following behind him, tried to hold him back. I won't try to repeat the words that were spoken; the blood froze in my veins, so terribly did the man speak, his words were so raw and unspeakably mean that I could only partially understand them. All I remember is his last sentence, 'Take her, James, take the prostitute, and if she is prickly, give her a kick. I will sell you the woman for a thousand pounds. As you know, she is worth the price, and you are very fond of her. For all she can to . . .'

I jumped up.

Major Johnson had also risen.

I tried to escape from the room, but Weston stepped in the way—I

121

still remember feeling his breath smelling of whiskey in my face, seeing his staring, bloodshot eyes in front of me and hearing his hoarse, rough voice. And then it happened. He attacked me and I . . . I think I grabbed a steel paper knife lying on the table and drove it into his chest. He screamed and the world went black; I fell to the ground, unconscious.

When I returned to my senses, I was lying on the sofa in the living room. The major stood bent over me; he was pale, but very calm.

"Mrs. Weston," he said, "rely on me, no harm shall come to you. Believe me, trust me! It was me who killed him, yes, it was me, you see, it was me!"

I didn't understand him at first, but soon learned what had happened, learned it, while I trembled with fright and agitation, and in my agitation, I accepted what the others suggested. So I became my brother's accomplice and plunged myself into all the misfortune from which only you alone, you, the only one whom I love, can liberate me."

At this point, the judge broke off the interrogation, considering the witness's overwrought state, and postponed it to the following morning. It was now eleven o'clock at night.

Interrogation closed—witness dismissed—court recessed.

***

Continuation of the previous interrogation.

On July 13, at eleven o'clock in the morning, the court reassembled in the same place. Amy Weston, free from coercion and influence, reappeared and continued as follows:

"With the help of a sleeping powder, I spent the night after the event in peace. And on the next day, contrary to all expectations, I was well enough to attend the discussions between my brother and Major Johnson. And then it turned out that, in infamy, my brother was not only equal to Weston but even his superior. Major Johnson insisted that he should have killed my husband himself and agreed to take all responsibility. But my brother tried to make it clear to him that this step could only ruin him and would bring no benefit. I felt sick and weak, shuddering, as a woman, at the thought of police and jail, and my brother made full use of my weakness. He behaved like a true villain; he forged a plan to continue Weston's cruelty after his death. After

122

disposing of the body in the cellar, he brought the major completely under his influence, partly by implying that I would be softened by his knightly behavior, partly by pointing to the certain prospect of being publicly involved in a scandalous affair. He even managed to persuade the major to disappear in name and to spread the rumor that he had gone to Burma. And all of this my brother didn't do for my sake, but— as it turned out later—to impose his authority on the major, and to continue using him as a gold mine just as he had done during Weston's lifetime.

And so began that hateful life, which didn't end until the day my brother drowned."

When asked by the judge, the witness stated that she knew with certainty that she and not the major had dealt the fatal blow to Weston. Although she had noticed the cat's disappearance, in the scurry of subsequent events, she had paid little attention to this fact, until her recent visit to the house and the explanation of the cat's liberation from the cellar. The witness admits that the path taken by the judge in his investigation was the right one, but she declares that she has made this open and full confession only out of love for him, in whose hands she also lays her future fate.

With reference to Miss Derry, she explains when asked that she doesn't know this lady, but only knows that she has a strong affection for the major. She knows Miss Derry has been investigating the major's whereabouts, and that this was one of the reasons why the major took the name of the deceased—Weston. With reference to the major, the witness declared that despite his behavior toward her, his weakness of character, and his irregular habits regarding money matters, she didn't consider him a truly bad man, and that in this one case he had indeed shown her a certain chivalry, which was, however, undermined again by his subsequent weakness and his indulgence towards her brother. She explained, concerning her brother, that he was in every respect a corrupt and vicious man, and that she had only obeyed him for fear of being involved in a public scandal that might have led to the discovery of the murder.

After this, the witness stated that she threw herself on the mercy of the court and would comply with all the measures the judge thought fit. The interrogation closed at one o'clock.

Holger Nielsen.

Chapter Seven

"Please sit down, *Major*," said Doctor Koldby, "and you too, Miss Derry, please sit down."

Doctor Koldby had urgently invited both to appear in his hotel room, and they had quickly accepted his invitation.

"First of all, Major, I must tell you that today I received a letter from my friend Holger Nielsen in London. The letter bears the address: Cranbourne Grove 48, the tenants of which, as Miss Derry knows, are Mr. Nielsen and myself. The cat found in the house, as you, Miss Derry, already know, belongs to Mrs. Weston; the corpse found in the cellar of the house, about which *you*, Major, are fully informed, is that of Mr. Weston. I think, Miss Derry, you will now give up all attempts to assist your former fiancé. I know everything now, and I believe it is time for you both to lay down your arms. The wisest thing you can do, Major, is to acknowledge that you are Major Johnson, and to get Mrs. Weston out of your head. And as for you, Miss Derry, it's best to refer to Major Johnson—not Mr. Weston. I consider it my duty to read you an excerpt from my friend's report and I ask that you listen to me closely."

Thereupon Koldby read a carefully prepared outline of Nielsen's documents.

Miss Derry turned pale and finally burst into tears, while Major Johnson's face turned a yellowish tint.

After Koldby had finished his lecture, he looked up questioningly. "Well, Major, are you prepared to be escorted to London by the police?"

The major seemed ready to explode, but Koldby took no notice and continued, "So you are not prepared. Well, I would like to avoid this as well. On the other hand, are you inclined to be escorted by Miss Derry to London? It seems to me that she deserves your respect."

Miss Derry blushed, and the major stole a glance at the pretty girl.

Koldby went on calmly, "I ask you, Major, to be so good as to confirm the truth of what Mrs. Weston has testified, that is, to sign this statement here, which I have taken the liberty of writing on your behalf. I will read it to you:

"I, the signee, James Johnson, hereby declare that I have been an eyewitness to the following events: On the evening of April 26 this year at Cranbourne Grove, 48, London, the late Mr. Weston, while in a drunken state, violently attacked his wife, Amy Weston, née Throgmorton. In self-defense, she reached for a paper knife that happened to be present and inflicted a wound upon him; he died as a result. And I declare my willingness to repeat and affirm, under oath, this testimony on demand, whenever and wherever it may be required, before any Danish or English court."

The major raged, "That would mean nothing but scandal and jail."

Koldby shrugged, "Yes, I can't help you with that. You have made an unforgivable mistake and must take the consequences. However, nothing prevents you from giving your statement to the local magistrate. I don't believe that you would be arrested because you haven't been charged with a crime. Or you can do it tomorrow at the probate court . . . you'll be completely released."

The major hesitated, "No," he said then, "no! You can have me arrested—but you can't make me live with the shame!"

Miss Derry looked at him miserably and began to cry again.

"Well," said Koldby, "you think that such a step would bring you death as well as much grief for this young lady; and by no means can Mr. Weston return to life. Very correct, quite my opinion as well. But you forget that in the cellar of the house at Cranbourne Grove lies a corpse that may be discovered at any moment. In that case, the whole matter—whatever we may do now, and whatever we may want—would be stirred up again. Especially now that Throgmorton's affairs are to be probated, it is likely that the house will be placed in the hands of the creditors," Koldby bluffed, "and then the discovery of the secret is only a matter of time."

"Yes," said the major, "but we must postpone that for a while, until I am safely gone. Let's see if they can find me!"

"That is excellent, for you!" cried the doctor. "But Mrs. Weston is entitled to your testimony. One imagines she might prefer not to be convicted and sentenced for a murder that never happened, especially as she is not guilty of the only crime that *has* been committed—the concealment of the body."

"Nor am I," said the major. "Throgmorton did that alone."

"Throgmorton is dead," replied the doctor shortly, "and besides, you have been living under the name of the murdered man for several months."

"And for *that* reason I will indeed go into exile," said the major.

"And I'll go with you," said Miss Derry cheerfully, immediately blushing.

Doctor Koldby smiled, "That's all very pretty, Miss Derry. I admire you and would gladly help the major, though you both tried to throw sand in my eyes. But only if I am able to justify myself with Nielsen and Mrs. Weston."

"Doctor," said Miss Derry, embarrassed, "the major will sign the first part of your statement; then we shall move away. If Mrs. Weston is brought to court later, I think the court will act justly."

"Possibly," replied the doctor, "but not at all likely."

"Then I would let the corpse lie quietly in the cellar and leave the courts untroubled," cried Miss Derry indignantly.

"I agree!" said the doctor. "If we can. Without doubt. But look— Nielsen may have other ideas; he's a legal scholar, a criminologist, a philosopher . . ."

"But he loves her!"

"Yes, Miss Derry—love is undoubtedly an unusually fine thing—but first and foremost come one's duties toward society."

"I would have just burnt the body—why didn't Throgmorton do that?"

"I would have preferred nothing better than if he had, though cremations in South Kensington may, on occasion, attract attention. But if he had, Miss Derry, I doubt you would have ever found your fiancé again. But, well, sign the first part of that statement, Major. Of course, it is completely useless, as it hasn't gone through all the legal formalities. Then travel as far as you like."

This final proposal met with approval and the major signed the document.

"Just a minute," said the doctor, taking out the pocket watch he had found on the drowned man. "Look, this watch was actually the key to the puzzle. We found it on Throgmorton's body. Nielsen and I have engaged in some minor transgressions. Trifles, such as body-snatching and so on. But now you would do well to take the watch and leave the 1200 kroner to the probate court. If that is all you have on your conscience, then your conscience is of extraordinary purity."

And that was the end of the matter. The following day, "Mr. Weston" and Miss Derry left the place together—out from under the probate court's nose and to the great annoyance and excitement of the colony of gossiping tourists.

Chapter Eight

Løkken, 19 July 19–

Dear friend!

I have received the documents about the criminal case and see from them that you have given yourself the dignity of a judge. Well, that's your affair. But now you have appointed me as the appellate judge and tasked me to decide whether to pursue the case further or not. And that is going too far, dear friend. I will not do that! Thank heaven that I am not a lawyer, for I am the least suitable person imaginable for that. I protest against you imposing such a duty on me—I will not accept the appointment.

I think your interrogation was admirable, and, for my part, I succeeded in filling in the blanks that remained. If I were young, I would envy you, for youth and love are the only things that I envy others. Instead, I sit here on this rocky beach like an old gray crow and let my sad, croaking voice sound.

So, now you know everything about the affair. You have found out who the victim was—and who the killer is.

I have yet to report that Major Johnson has apparently taken pity on the faithful Amy No. 1, whom I have always admired, as far as I can admire any female.

And so, the whole story seems to be over, each of the characters has found resolution, as befits a story with a satisfying ending.

And yet the most important issue of all has remained unresolved: the corpse in the cellar!

A wise man, whose name I have forgotten, once said that it is the dead who rule over us mortals; they fill our earth with their bones, they live on and on in their works, they lay their bony hands on us—they command, and we must obey. That is true, because the dead made our laws, they set our course, they demand our obedience—they rule us.

The corpse in the cellar is still awaiting its resolution—You asked me what else is to be done. Yes, very kind of you to leave this decision to me. But I—I refuse to make this decision. I send the question back to you.

So, what?

Major Johnson and his Amy begged me urgently to spare them as regards the dead man. Although I protested for the sake of your Amy, I had to admit that it would be most foolish to destroy the lives of two people, possibly three, just to satisfy the so-called rights of this unmourned corpse. He was a rogue and got his due. He can't return to life, and as a dead man he has no claim to legal satisfaction. Only society, as all right-thinking people would say, only society has the right to demand satisfaction on his behalf. I have made the mistake of preventing the major and his Amy from being responsible to society; they have gone, I don't know where. Forgive me. A piece of paper on which he has attested a few words is all I could obtain; and though I am not a lawyer, I can see that this paper has no legal standing.

But if the dead man has let the major escape, he will only trap you and your Amy all the more surely. Fully within its rights, society will say *she* murdered him—will say *she* killed him, and *she* now must stand before society and justify her act. Only when a jury has acquitted her, will she be truly free—not before. The legal system we inherited from the dead requires it.

You know that as well as I do. You're a lawyer and you must understand that the corpse that's been in the cellar for the last three months has his rights and that society will vindicate them. You and Mrs. Weston must respect this and govern yourselves accordingly.

The body in the cellar must have a resolution. Miss Derry, in her female ignorance, suggested destroying it; she explained that it would have been best if Throgmorton had already burned it. That may be true, but as it is, the law must follow its usual course. All this means only, however, that your Amy would, at the very least, be questioned for murder, which would bring her much suffering and place her fate in the hands of a few indifferent men.

My dear friend, lawyer, pioneer of the judiciary, and whatever else you may call yourself, I said earlier that the story was over—and yet it has only just begun! Earlier, you wished to avoid the inconvenience of public prosecution; I myself encouraged you, and you successfully avoided it. It was hard, but it worked. Now, you are in exactly the same place you were at the beginning. And now, you can no longer avoid it, no, in fact, you can't.

I don't know what you think now—you are young and therefore

unstable. But for me, this case contains only one lesson: that we humans have surrounded ourselves for our protection with a so-called justice, which is just as much of our own creation as soldiers and guns are. It is something that has no inner justification, is not based on itself, so to speak, but only exists for our protection and—if we can't control it ourselves—it can become our enemy. Then the legal system resembles a sheep dog, who bares his teeth against the same flock that he guards. Therefore, don't talk about justice, but about a useful human institution which—as long as it is used only for its purpose—must also be defended.

The rights of the dead Mr. Weston are nothing in themselves; at most, one could say that society demands that the crime be pursued for society's own protection. I will leave it entirely up to you to judge this question. But one thing, even if you deny the question, always remains: Weston's dead body lies in the cellar of the house that is to accommodate your newly established happiness.

And it can't stay there.

I reject the duty you are imposing on me. I am unable to decide what you should do now; but I have these questions for you: Do you have the courage to continue, to complete Throgmorton's work? Do you have the courage—to spare your Amy—to make Weston's corpse—be it by burning, or by burial—disappear?"

Do you have the courage? Or do you condemn, together with the rest of honest humanity, the act that they would call a crime? Take note of this and admit that the affair is just beginning for you now. *Hic Rhodus—hic salta!*

Your friend, Jens Koldby.

P.S. In the heat of battle, I forgot something. Your report contains nothing regarding Amy's cat, although this is not an unimportant point. I have now learned from Miss Derry that the cat and the collar originally belonged to *her*. She received both from the major as a gift but sent both back to him later—to remind him of his loyalty. I hereby inform you that Miss Derry has now given the cat to *me*. So, she's *my* cat now, so please keep that in mind. Miss Derry, or rather Mrs. Johnson, as she is probably now called, says that the cat belongs to a very rare breed.

Chapter Nine

"Amy," said Nielsen, putting the doctor's letter on the table of the living room in which they sat, "here's a letter from Denmark from Doctor Koldby. I don't want to read it to you, because you don't know my friend and you would not be able to judge his words. However, he is right in what he writes—There is a corpse in the cellar of this house—a dead man who has found no resolution, no end. For three months he has waited calmly and patiently—waiting as only a dead man can wait. But now he requires our attention—demands it in the name of all the dead."

Amy looked up; there was concern in her eyes—worry and quiet terror. But she said nothing, and Nielsen went on, "When my friend and I discovered the dead body, we made an unusual decision. We acted on a theory—my theory—and every step we took based on that theory moved us in the right direction. At the same time, however, my gloomy gray theory was replaced by the bright green of life, and now life alone guides our actions; theory has receded. I have not forgotten for a moment that the deceased under our feet is demanding his rights—not the rights of the dead, but the rights of the living—the rights of our whole human society. I understand and acknowledge that society has a right to demand that no act by which a living person should die should be arbitrarily outside the law's jurisdiction. Can you see that, Amy? Do you feel, as I do, that we are unable to deny society its rights, that we—as the doctor writes—can't destroy all traces of what happened in this house?"

She didn't reply.

Nielsen continued, "There exists within us an instinct; it is innate and increases as we grow. Both of us may feel that your act was justified, that you didn't commit a crime when you stabbed Weston. And I also believe that if you stand face to face with the men whose duty is to judge us under the law of this land and tell them everything as you have told me, they would say, 'Go in peace. There is no crime here!' But you as well as I, we feel that we must face this judgment before we are absolved. Is this not true?"

131

"No," said Amy, "no. I've told you everything, and I shared everything because you wanted it that way. But you can't demand that I, the innocent, the defenseless, expose myself to a gaping crowd, subject myself to the dubious judgment of strangers who are indifferent to me. I feel that I am innocent—what weight should the judgment of others have? You understand me—and you say you love me!"

Nielsen knelt in front of her and took her hand.

"My Amy," he said, "you're right, you're really guiltless. But now get up, go down to the cellar, where the corpse lies. Destroy it, burn it— eradicate it. Do that, Amy, with your own hands."

Then she shuddered, bent her head over his shoulder, and he felt her tears on his cheek as she whispered, "I can't, Holger, I can't."

He kissed her eyes, "You see, Amy," he said sadly, "you can't do it, so it must not happen. I would do anything in the world for you, the hardest thing would seem easy to me if I did it for you. But I can't do this either, I can't do it. My inner voice guides all my actions. I feel what is right, and I feel what is wrong, and against this feeling all opposing thoughts and words die away. You and I, we are one; what I do for you, at the same time I do for me, and even if I could save you from conviction by doing this, I could still not do it."

"And if my life were at stake?" she whispered.

Nielsen looked up.

"Your life is out of the question, you know that. What you are afraid of is just the publicity that we would attract but that should be beneath us. We can't create rules that apply to all circumstances. The founders of religions have tried it, and the fallacy of every doctrine—the dispute between truth and falsehood—has always arisen. No, we humans have to look at everything in itself. Of course, this is not so deep, not so comprehensive, but it corresponds to human nature. The question we must face right now is not: Do you have the right to deceive society about what it is owed, if you can spare the one you love from society? We must not ask the question in this way, but we must make it less general. The question must be: Do I have the right to destroy Weston's body in order to protect you from interrogation? Only when people look at everything in detail, can we become clear about what our duty requires of us. Let preachers and poets speak of general rules—doctors, lawyers and everyday people have to take everything specifically, and so we must do here."

"Let's go abroad," Amy said, and Nielsen felt her shaking as she pressed her cheek against his again.

Nielsen shook his head, "We can't do that. There are only two choices: either speaking out freely and awaiting the judgment of society, or keeping silent, and destroying the corpse. You feel certain about what you should do—you feel as certain as I do. If we are wrong now, we will never be free; nobody can deny their inner voice with impunity. When an action has been taken, it can generally be defended; perhaps even this action, if it could not be undone, could be defended—but, well, no, the dead man lies in the cellar under our feet, he waits—he waits, and you and I, we must act now. We don't need a defense; what we need is a certainty that we have acted correctly. And you and I, we know how to act, to act correctly."

"And the shame?" she whispered, "The shame of standing before all these people face to face! O Holger, Holger, you must be able to feel how terrible that would be."

"Amy," Nielsen said, putting his arm around her, "I once gave a lecture about crime and punishment to an association of young socialists. One of them asked me if I thought that any trial should be publicly held, and I answered in the affirmative. But, nevertheless, I added, I could well understand that a woman who has been injured by a man may claim that the public shouldn't be involved, because the shame would fall on both the innocent and the guilty. And the young worker answered me, 'Shouldn't we educate society, to only feel shame where there is an action that really deserves shame?' And I said nothing, for the young man was right."

"Only the poorest live so close together that have nothing to hide," said Amy. "You must understand, Holger, that I, who have lived so far away from the world, feel clearly that the shame would fall upon me even though I am only the victim. I beg you, Holger, do it for my sake, for the sake of our love!"

Nielsen had risen; she also got up and wrapped her arms around his neck.

"Save me, Holger, save me for the last time from that terrible man and from the evil that he can still do to me."

Nielsen broke free; he took both her hands and kissed them, one after the other, then he kissed her forehead, eyes, and mouth.

"Amy," he said, "I'm at your side. If I refused to listen to my inner voice, then not only would I be acting against myself, but also against you. Come, today will go to court, and you will see, as soon as we have told the truth, the burden will be gone from us. We won't do it because society rules us with its laws, but because it accords with the innate nature that sustains the interactions between human and human, each for themselves and for all others."

***

Then the front doorbell rang. Moments later, Madame Sivertsen entered.

"Mr. Nielsen, here's a telegram for you."

Nielsen took and read it; it was from Doctor Koldby.

Amy kept her eyes fixed on him, her cheeks glowing, and in a hoarse voice she exclaimed, "Before we do anything, Holger—talk to him first—talk to him or let me talk to him."

Nielsen smiled, "Do you know what he's said? Only this, 'Meet me at the South Weston Hotel in Southampton at seven-thirty tomorrow night.'"

Amy grabbed his hand and pleaded, "Do that, Holger, do that before you do anything else."

And the next morning, Nielsen packed his suitcase and asked Amy to accompany him to Southampton.

Chapter Ten

Madame Sivertsen stood rigid as she opened the door and saw Doctor Koldby outside.

"Heavens! You're here, Doctor? And Mr. Nielsen just drove to Southampton to meet you there today. The lady also went with him. You know the lady?"

"Yes, I know the lady," said the doctor, who spoke rather hastily and seemed most excited. "I had my reasons for getting Nielsen and the lady to Southampton. And now I would like to ask you, Madame Sivertsen, to also go there at once, this evening, and to give this letter to Mr. Nielsen. A train leaves at six o'clock from Waterloo Station; if you get ready right away, you can still catch it. You would do me a great service if you travel immediately—a very great service."

Madame Sivertsen stepped back in astonishment, but, as already mentioned, she was accustomed to following orders, and at six o'clock she was off to Southampton on the express train.

The doctor remained alone in the house. He sat down in the dining room—took the cat in his lap and made a small speech to her.

"Amy's Puss," he said, "you're a miserable cat that nobody cares about. And yet you are the one who is aware of many things that—if they come to light—would cause the whole world to proclaim, in their simplicity, that you were sent straight from heaven with your silver necklace, so that what was done in secret would be brought openly into the light of day. I don't want to take that glory from you, Puss. I am a poor man who does his best to act humanely. I ignore generalities and stick only to the details. And responsibility, little puss, I take on myself. I've always done that and will continue to do so. But you and I, we have to stick together. Otherwise this will not work."

Puss nuzzled and purred. And Doctor Koldby sat deep in thought for a long time. Then he pulled himself together, jumped up, and got to work . . .

***

135

Madame Sivertsen met Nielsen and Mrs. Weston at the hotel in Southampton. They were waiting for the doctor and were most surprised to see Madame Sivertsen instead.

Nielsen opened the letter hesitantly. The letter read:

"Dear Nielsen!

"Return to London tomorrow morning, because you can't come sooner. Bring Madame Sivertsen back with you and your heart's chosen one. Take my best wishes on your way into the sunshine. I loved you—very much; and now you are separated from my life. Only accept this one piece of advice from me. Stay away from cursed justice with its laws; give it up. Only fools can think that justice follows rules; only fools believe in a rational justice, which in truth is nothing but a miserable process of checking boxes. Look for truth and happiness in life. Look for it with *her*.

Be happy, Nielsen. Make your home in Cranbourne Grove because it is a pretty, comfortable house, though it contains some memories. And as for the rooms beneath the house, you can quietly lead your bride down and show her all of them, for there is nothing left to frighten her; what was once is no more—that has been my work, and my gift to you! Miss Derry gave me the idea. Now it is done, and no one in the world can undo it.

The major and Miss Derry have gone off to seek their fortune. Help them. This is a beginning of which we humans need not to be ashamed. I will also go away. I don't want to see you again for the time being—maybe a good while later. I only want to tell you that I am not going out into the world alone; I shall be accompanied by the one remaining player in this game who could still reveal your secret: Amy's cat. Good luck for the future!

Your friend, Jens Koldby."

***

In the western part of Cornwall, between granite cliffs and moorland, lies Sennen Cove—a small fishing village. To the west of it, the cliffs of Pedn-men-du have piled up against the waves of the Atlantic Ocean, which crash against them.

It was here that a foreign painter arrived one afternoon in July; he was a Dane and took up residence in a small cottage near the cliffs.

His luggage arrived in a cart from Penzance—apart from a travel plaid suitcase, an easel, and the paint tubes, it consisted of an immense box, which, he said, contained a sculpture he had done, for he was also active in the field of sculpture. It was the statue of a young woman, his favorite work, his life's masterpiece.

The painter was accompanied by a well-fed gray cat, whose name was Amy's Puss. The inhabitants of the village were already accustomed to the visits of such "painter-fellows" and took no notice of them; they considered them all to be pagans and invariably mad and found no reason to distinguish the newcomer from the rest.

The big box in the cottage had a room of its own and was never unpacked.

One day, however, when a fierce northwest storm raged against the cliffs, the painter hired a fisherman and a two-wheeled cart, and with the help of both, brought the box to the farthest end of a cliff and threw it down with his own hands into the roaring depths. The waves splashed high, as the box hit the water before it sunk into the depths to the rocky bottom.

This adventure only encouraged the fishermen in their opinion that this painter-fellow was crazy—perhaps a little more than the others of his kind—but the event was soon forgotten, and the sunken statue remained among the wreckage on the seabed along with other remnants from the time of pirates.

Doctor Koldby soon left the village and continued on his journey to distant shores—and Amy's cat moved with him.

Chapter Eleven

It was Mr. Sydney Armstrong who sold the house at Cranbourne Grove 48. A young painter bought it because he liked it very much and it was not expensive. Mrs. Nielsen, who was traveling abroad with her husband, Holger Nielsen, a young Danish jurist, had wanted to sell it.

The two traveled across the sea and visited the New World, where Mrs. Nielsen saw her childhood home in the West Indies again. And there they found summer and sunshine and were happy in their love.

Amy didn't quite understand how it had come about—and she didn't want to ask—but one summer's night under the deep blue skies of the tropics, they talked. "Holger," she said, "why were you so serious about what you said, and I cried and begged you—but you don't seem to remotely think of it now?"

Holger put his arm around her and said with a smile, "Did you believe I would run to the police and say, 'There was a dead man in my cellar once, and now he's not there anymore; because Doctor Koldby has removed him unlawfully?'"

Amy took a step back.

"What? For the sake of your friend, you would stand against justice, but my requests were not enough to hold you back when you spoke of the rights of society?"

"Foolish girl," said Nielsen, "have you forgotten the inner voice, the voice I spoke about? Now it has become quiet, correct? And you know why—Because we humans can't expect an answer to every question we ask. The voice in us only speaks about that which is real. If Jens Koldby acted as he did, he must have also justified it to his own inner voice—he has taken the question away from us. You can feel that, can you not? I can only learn *one* lesson from this case, namely that we, who deal with so-called law and so-called justice, must give up any hope of finding a golden rule. There are no such rules, but only a series of individual cases, which must be judged one by one. Every human must do his utmost to act *as* righteously as his heart dictates, and this series of righteous acts constitutes the whole of the law."

Amy didn't quite understand him.

But he took her in his arms and said laughingly, "Of course that is only a doctrine; but that's not all! I also keep the memory with me; I won you, and I will keep you through the rights of love."

***

So, they found happiness and life together.

The Publisher

No, this is not another chapter of *The Man in the Cellar*. Since you like mysteries, we've included here a short story from our book *The Adventures of Dagobert Trostler, Vienna's Sherlock Holmes* by Balduin Groller. We hope you enjoy it. But first, a word from our sponsor, which is us!

Kazabo Publishing is a new idea in the literary world. Our motto is, "Every Book a Best Seller . . . <u>Guaranteed!</u>" And we mean it. Our mission is to find best-selling books from around the world that, for whatever reason, have not been published in English. Palle Rosenkrantz's novels are very popular in Europe but very few have been published in English. Why? We don't know. But we think you will agree that they should have been. And now they are.

We have found there are also many contemporary writers who are very popular in their own countries but who have not made it into English. We think this is a real shame so we are working to bring those books and those authors to you.

When you visit Kazabo.com (our website!), we hope you will always discover something new, either a book from a favorite author you didn't know existed or a completely new author with a fresh perspective from a country you admire. We promise you that everything you see with the Kazabo name – even authors you have never heard of – will be a best-seller; maybe in Italy, maybe in Japan, maybe in 1902, but a best seller. We hope you enjoy reading these literary gems as much as we enjoy finding them and bringing them to you.

But enough about us. Here is one of Dagobert Trostler's adventures entitled "The Fine Cigars."

Thanks for reading!

The Kazabo Team
Kazabo.com

The Fine Cigars
By Balduin Groller

1.

After dinner, they went into the smoking room. This was an iron law, and could not be otherwise. The two gentlemen might have preferred to sit at the table to smoke their cigars in comfort, having enjoyed the culinary masterpieces, but that was not possible, absolutely not possible. They had known this for a long time, and now the departure and exodus seemed to them quite self-evident. The beautiful housewife had made it so. In her house, smoking was allowed only in the smoking room. There, she even took part occasionally and smoked a cigarette herself in company, but for all the other rooms—she imposed this—there was the strictest ban on smoking.

Mrs. Violet Grumbach, like any self-respecting person, took as much care over her person as her apartment. Just as her outward appearance was staged with every conceivable care, with taste and good calculation, so too was the apartment. The decor was modern and expensive, everything was spick-and-span and positively sparkled in cleanliness. Yet, it is sometimes still said that former artists generally don't make good housewives!

Frau Violet had been an actress. Not one of the very foremost, but certainly one of the prettiest. Even now, all that was true! She was an exceptionally attractive woman. A little under medium height, her figure pleasingly roundish and full, already considerably more developed than at the time of her active artistry. The pale blonde hair, always elaborately ordered, bright, sparkling gray eyes, delicately drawn, soft red lips, and a piquant, pert little snub nose which still gave the round little face a kind of childish expression. All in all, a very pleasant ensemble.

At meals, she loved always to appear in a specially chosen attire. There were no children in the house, so she had time to enhance life, and overall, she had a very good way of enhancing life, indeed. She adorned herself and her surroundings. It is thus understandable that she didn't want to expose her curtains, her lace and doilies, her ceilings,

141

and her silk carpets to the evil effects of tobacco.

Today, only one guest was present, the old friend of the house, Dagobert Trostler, and he was so at home at the Grumbach's that absolutely no bother was made on his account. If Frau Violet had once again attended elaborately to her attire, it was not actually meant for him. Once upon a time, it was customary even when she dined alone with her husband. Now, at the very most, some nuances were added on account of the guest. Thus, the heart-shaped cutout of her white lace blouse, which gave the observer some views and insights, and the half-length lace sleeves, which gave the plumpish forearms that delicately tapered to fine wrists and pretty little hands the desired scope.

Mr. Andreas Grumbach, owner of a large and very lucrative jute weaving mill, president of the General Construction Company Bank, and also bearer of numerous titles and honors, was considerably older than his wife—around twenty years or so— and though one is denied calculating the age of ladies with too much brutal accuracy, it may be revealed with him. He might have seen fifty-three or fifty-four springs, but he looked even older than he was. His beautiful dark-brown, smooth-brushed hair proved nothing. He could have had his hair dressed professionally. His sideburns already shimmered strongly silver, and yet his chin had been shaved in the attempt to look a little younger and not to let the silvery blessing grow excessively.

Dagobert Trostler, his old friend, had by no means been sanguine when Grumbach, pursuing the late stirrings of love, had brought home the actress Violet Moorlank as his wedded spouse about six years ago. But nothing could be done about it, and finally Dagobert was proven wrong all along. A quite acceptable and respectable household developed of it. The marriage turned into a very happy one.

Dagobert himself had remained a bachelor. He was a fully-fledged man-about-town with a noticeably thinning crown and a St Peter's style tuft of hair. His Socratic face was enlivened by two dark, expressive eyes. Now he had only two great passions, music and criminology. His great fortune allowed him to devote himself to these two very divergent hobbies without anxiety. He had an enjoyable and creative relationship with music. His friends claimed that it was the stronger of his two talents. He, too, had known Violet when she was still a member of the theater, and when one or another of her roles required that she sing some songs, he was the one who had rehearsed her. As an amateur, of course. He remained an amateur, passionate dilettante, gentleman-rider in all the fields of activity in which he was engaged. He had, however, had some musical success with that arrangement. Indeed, in this way, he sometimes succeeded in smuggling one or another of his own compositions into the public as contributions.

As far as his criminological inclinations were concerned, they first expressed themselves in the fact that he leaned toward talking about murder-robberies and halfway respectable embezzlements. He was convinced he could have been a first-rate detective inspector, and stiffly asserted that if worst came to the worst, he would be well able to earn his bread as a detective. His friends made fun of him for it. Not that they would have doubted his talent. He had often enough provided convincing proof of that. But they found his passion for making unnecessary trouble for himself peculiar. For his hobby brought him not only numerous inconveniences, but also occasionally entangled him in really quite dangerous situations. If there was a crowd of people somewhere, he was certainly there, too, but not with an interest in the current proceedings, whatever they might be. He would watch out for pickpockets and endeavored to observe them at work and catch them in the act. For this reason, he was not infrequently involved in risky complications, but he still succeeded in delivering many a pilferer into police hands. He also loved to do research into dark crimes on his own initiative, and so it was that he brought all sorts of trouble down on his own head, had dealings in court at every moment, or was summoned to the police, to whom his private efforts had sometimes become uncomfortable. But all this gave him pleasure. He was an amateur after all.

So, after dinner, one went to the smoking room.

The two gentlemen sat down at the little smoker's table near the window. Frau Violet took a seat on a small, padded bench—a very charming piece of furniture—which stretched from the high and finely structured chimney to the door, and there filled the space very becomingly. The fireplace stood in a corner, creating a very cozy little spot.

Grumbach took a cigar box from the smoking table, not at random. There were several of them there, and he had chosen carefully. He opened it and was about to pass the cigars to Dagobert as he trimmed.

"I don't know," he said thoughtfully, "there must still be a

143

connoisseur in my house for precisely this sort of cigar. It would not be bad taste: they cost a florin apiece!"

"Do you notice disappearances?" asked Dagobert.

"I think I notice them," replied Grumbach.

"Nothing is stolen in our house," said Frau Violet, defending her honor as housewife.

"Thank God, no!" Grumbach replied. "And yet—certainly, I can't state it for a fact—but it seems to me as if only two cigars were missing from the top yesterday, and today there are eight or nine missing."

"Your own fault," remarked Dagobert. "You must simply keep them under lock and key!"

"One should be able to leave a thing lying around free in one's own home!"

"Perhaps you are mistaken?" suggested Frau Violet.

"It would not be impossible, but I don't believe it. Well, it isn't a misfortune precisely, but it is disturbing."

"It should not be difficult to get to the bottom of the matter, however," remarked Dagobert, in whom the detective passion began to stir.

"The simplest thing will be to follow your advice, Dagobert. Lock it. That's the best protection."

"That would not be interesting enough for me," was the reply. "You must catch the marten!"

"Am I supposed to be on the lookout for days on end? It'll cost me a lot less if I buy a few more cigars."

"But you must know who has access to the room."

"I stand for my servant. He takes nothing!"

"And I for my maid," Frau Violet added hurriedly. "She's been with me since I was a child, and not a pin has ever gone missing!"

"Even better," continued Dagobert. "Do you think there are daily disappearances?"

"God forbid! That's all I need! Last week I thought I had noticed it, and then perhaps in the previous week too."

The subject dropped. They spoke a little while more about the events of the day that occupied public opinion. Then the host and hostess rose to make their final preparations to attend the opera. It was their day for the box, Wednesday, and Dagobert was supposed to make one of the party, as usual. Such an old acquaintance and familiar friend of the house could be left alone for a little quarter of an hour, without awkwardness.

Frau Violet, joking, said that it must even be welcome to remain alone for a while, since he could now cogitate undisturbed on the gloomy problem of where the disappearing cigars had got to. He would surely work it out, as a master detective!

This mocking appeal was not necessary to remind him of his hobby. He had already quietly decided to discover the perpetrator, and now he welcomed the chance to look around the scene of the crime undisturbed. The case was in fact quite insignificant, but what does an amateur not do to stay in training? He takes an opportunity like this.

When he was alone, he sat down in his armchair and began to think, for the story was not quite so simple. The last offense had been committed the day before. He assessed the cigar box and the smoking table. There was nothing to discover. It was simply disgusting what kind of cleanliness prevailed in the house, how things were tidied up and wiped down daily! How was a person expected to discover a fingerprint on the wood frame of a smoking table with a red fabric border? The frame probably was not dusty yesterday either, and since then it had been ridiculously wiped and polished again. How was a man supposed to make fingerprint studies?

Okay. Forget that.

Four electric lamps now lit the room. He turned the other eight on with a knob. Radiant light filled the room, and now he examined further. He paced the room in all directions, and sent a searching glance everywhere, unable to find any clue.

Then he sat again at the smoking table. It was clear that this had to form the center of the inquiries. However much he peered, no trace and no *corpus delicti* was discovered, But, just as he was about to resume his pacing, he noticed something. Nestled in the narrow gap between the cloth and wood frame of the smoking table, and projecting over it, was a hair, dark and shiny, not long—perhaps five centimeters, straightened—but it had the tendency to form a circle.

Dagobert ran his hand over the cloth, the frame, and the gap where the hair was. The hair bent and remained stuck. So, it had also been able to withstand polishing and dusting. On the other hand, the way things were cleaned here—absolutely disgusting—it was probably safe to assume that this resistance would hardly be permanent. Multiple attacks would probably sweep the hair away. It was quite possible, indeed probable, that it only got stuck yesterday.

He thought for a moment about calling in the servant to ascertain whether someone who was not part of the household had entered the room today, perhaps to get out of him who had been there yesterday, but he pushed the thought away immediately. Of course he wanted to, had to spy, but not with the servants! That could lead to foolish talk, and he was guilty of a certain regard for the house of his best friend.

So, he lifted the hair with his fingertips and put it with extreme care in his billfold. Then he continued his research. He had a good look around the entire room again. There was hardly anything more to be learned. The lighting was so bright that he was unlikely to miss anything. Up on the smooth, polished surface of the black-marble fireplace mantle, he noticed a small, dark lump interrupting the sharp straight line. Was it worth examining? For a detective, everything is worth it, anything can be worthwhile.

He pulled up a leather chair and climbed on it. A cigar butt, about four centimeters long. A very light layer of dust on the polished ledge. If only the housewife knew! It had not been wiped today. The servant had made himself comfortable. Probably he only wiped every second or third day. The thin layer of dust was not older than that. Neither was the stub. A smoker can judge these things. And another thing: there was no trace of a hand or finger on the dust surface. The ledge, therefore, had not been dusty when the cigar butt was put there. So, it had been set there yesterday.

Dagobert examined the stub. It came from the type of cigar in question.

Now Dagobert got off the chair, put the carefully wrapped stub in his pocket, extinguished the surplus lamps, and then, when the time came, went to the opera.

2.

Grumbach had already forgotten the whole cigar matter the next day. The busy factory owner and merchant had other things to think about. He didn't come back to it later, because there was no reason to do so. The matter was still not done with, however.

Dagobert let almost a whole week pass before he returned to Grumbach's home. The last time he had been there on a Wednesday, and he didn't show up again until the following Tuesday evening. Frau

Violet received him in the smoking room. Dinner was over, and with the coffee he was supposed to have with her, she liked to smoke a cigarette.

"Have I arrived inopportunely, ma'am?" he began the conversation.

"You are always welcome, Herr Dagobert," she replied amiably, but she seemed to be a little bit sheepish as she sat down on the fireplace bench.

"I only meant," he went on innocently, "because I had anticipated that I would not meet your husband at home."

"Certainly, Tuesday is his club day. He is never at home then. All the more pleasant for me to have company."

"It would have been possible, however, that madame had already provided herself with different society, and that I might only have been an inconvenience."

"You are never an inconvenience, Herr Dagobert," she assured him eagerly, then steered the conversation a different direction, by attacking his weak side and beginning to tease him with his detective passion.

"Now, have you not discovered the nefarious cigar marten yet?" she asked with cheerful mockery.

"Do not mock too early, madame."

"My God, a few cigars can easily go missing without one knowing where they've gone. You should simply not investigate. The next thing will be to suspect the servant. He is certainly innocent, but once suspicion is aroused—my husband is very strict—the poor devil could easily lose his livelihood."

"We shall soon see for ourselves," replied Dagobert, pressing the electric switch.

Frau Violet was frightened by his forwardness and made a movement to hold him back, but it was already too late. Within seconds, the servant was in the room awaiting orders.

"You, my dear Franz," began Dagobert, "Will you be so good as to get me a cab, in about an hour."

"Very well, sir!"

"Here, dear friend, for your effort a fine cigar!" Dagobert reached for the little box.

"I beg your pardon, sir, I don't smoke."

"Oh, nonsense, Franz," said Dagobert. "Now get out your cigar box. We want to fill it properly." And he now reached into the little

147

box with his whole hand.

Franz laughed broadly at the joke, and assured him that he was not a smoker.

"Well, that's all right," remarked Dagobert affably, "then we will still settle things between ourselves. You should not miss out."

The servant bowed and left the room noiselessly.

"You see, madame," resumed Dagobert. "It was not him."

Now it was up to Frau Violet to laugh brightly.

"If that's your entire trick, Dagobert, then you had better go to the bottom of the class! Indeed, I don't say that it was him—it certainly was not. But even if he had been guilty, do you really believe he would fallen into this clumsy trap?"

"Who says, Frau Violet, that this is all I have up my sleeve? I only wanted to demonstrate to you that he could not be the culprit."

"Because you believe everything he says at once. You are naïve, Dagobert."

"It was pointless for me to summon him. I only wanted to accomplish his salvation before you. Actually, in quite a superfluous way, for you, too, are convinced of his innocence, and thus we could regard the matter as closed."

"Dagobert, you know more than you say."

"I will tell you everything, if it interests you, my dear."

"I am very interested."

"Would it be better not to talk about it at all any longer?"

"Indeed, why should it be better, Dagobert?"

"I just thought—because I know everything."

"All the better. Let me hear what you have found out."

"It is, of course, possible that I am mistaken in the details, then you will be able to correct me."

"I?" She looked at him magnificently.

"You, madame. It is also possible that I will make a fool of myself—I don't believe it, but it's possible. You must take into account that I have been solely dependent on my reasoning, and I have, quite naturally, scorned to pump your servants for information."

"Not such a long introduction, Dagobert. Get to the point, please."

"Fine, I'll show my cards. You remember, my dearest, that last Wednesday I heard about the disappearances for the first time. Five minutes later I had the exact description of the person."

148

"How did you get that, then?"

"The exact description of the person, the smoker. I think we will stay with this designation and avoid the odious expression thief or even cigar thief. The cigars, indeed, were not stolen, but merely smoked without the master knowing it. The smoker is, therefore, a tall young man, a head taller than I am, with a well-groomed black beard and splendid teeth."

"How do you know?"

"I'll tell you everything, madame. By the way, I hope to see the correctness of the personal description I've supplied strikingly confirmed today. Namely, I am counting on the fact that the excellent young man will soon grant us the honor of his company. I have already filled the box with his favorite cigars."

Then the door opened, and the servant entered with the message that the carriage had been ordered for the gracious lord, and that it would drive up punctually at the appointed time. Then he addressed to the housewife the question of whether he was now "allowed to go." Permission was granted, and he withdrew with a submissive bow of thanks.

"Franz is actually a theater fiend," explained Frau Violet. "Once a week he must go to the theater, and I prefer to give him Tuesday evenings off, when my husband isn't at home, and he can be most easily dispensed with."

"Oh, I see," replied Dagobert thoughtfully. "Well, that is indeed fair enough."

"Do not let that distract you, dear Dagobert," continued Frau Violet. "You owe me the explanation of how you got to that description of the person."

"I had a few minutes to investigate on Wednesday, when you and your husband retired to prepare for the theater. The matter might perhaps have become difficult if I had not found any clues on the scene."

"And you found some?"

"Yes. A hair in the gap of the smoking table, and a cigar stub on the mantelpiece."

"But they could have been lying here and there for a long time!"

"I had my reasons to believe that they were actually *corpora delicti* and had only arrived there the day before. I then examined the two objects

149

at home, the hair microscopically."

"And the result?"

"A perfectly satisfying one. The hair pointed to a perpetrator with a beautiful black beard. Natural black, no trace of artificial dye. So, an old man isn't our smoker. I can even say that it is a young man. For the hair was soft, pliant and supple. Not exactly the first fluff, but still delicate. It would have been coarser and more bristly, if a razor had prevailed there for many years past. The young man also puts something on his beard, for under the microscope the hair showed a trace of Brilliantine. This is a quite harmless, cosmetic remedy, but one must be a little vain to apply it. As you know the perpetrator, my dear, you will indeed be able to judge whether my assumption is correct or erroneous."

"I think you've gotten carried away by an obsession."

"Possibly. But that isn't important. Let's move on. Up here, on the fireplace ledge, lay the cigar stub."

"To what conclusions did it lead you?"

"First of all, I was pleased to see that the cigar type was the right one. Further conclusions were self-evident. Now allow me to return to your servant. I mention here in conclusion something which I had assumed from the beginning. Not for no reason did I call him in. You should take another look at him. So, the man is blond, and his face, as befitting a proper servant, also serving at the table, is shaved smooth. In addition, not befitting a proper servant, and as you could see for yourself when he grinned so kindly at us, he has very bad teeth. Finally, you could see that his stature is a rather small one. He's a little smaller than I am, and we have established that the unknown perpetrator has a black beard, has very good teeth, and is a head taller than I am."

"We have not yet established this at all!"

"Then we'll do so immediately. The tip of the cigar had not been cut off with a knife, but had been bitten off cleanly and smoothly. This means good teeth. Now we've got that straight. Now his unusual height must be proven. Nothing easier than that. Let us reproduce the situation, my gracious one—actually not necessary at all. Because it is already established. You at your preferred spot, I leaning against the fireplace opposite you, at a respectful distance, but still close enough for our conversation. The prospect, which I enjoy almost from a bird's eye view, is an enchanting one—calm yourself, Frau Violet, there will

150

be no need for violence—indeed, an adorable one. I would not leave my happy observer post on a mere whim. But if I had to put away a cigar, I would have to go to the smoker's table, where the ashtrays stand, because I could not reach the ledge. It would be too high for me! There, now I have justified the person's description. Is it correct, my dear?"

"It is true," admitted Frau Violet, laughing. "I compliment you, Herr Dagobert. You are a terrible man, and I can see that it will be for the best if I make a comprehensive confession, or else God knows what you will believe in the end!"

"No confessions! I reject them. Confessions—of course I speak quite academically—can also be wrong. There have been legal executions on the basis of false confessions, and nothing gets my blood up more than the thought of a judicial murder. Besides, I don't need the confession. It cannot help me anymore. I am only an examining magistrate here, and I make no rulings. My task was to clarify the facts and prove the perpetrators. Whether this is confessed or denied in the final negotiation, I am not concerned."

"Good, so let us hear more!"

"So, I had to deduce further. The tall young man with the beautiful beard and the good teeth smoked his cigar here in your presence and provided you company. He chatted with you as I am now speaking with you. There could be no special secret behind it."

"Thank God that you don't think me capable of that at least, Dagobert!"

"That could not be behind it. We have known each other long enough—you are a clever woman. You know what's at stake, and you don't do stupid things."

"I thank you for your trust in my honor!"

"My trust is rock-solid, no less so my respect. But it isn't just that. I have open eyes and good ears. I myself would have noticed something, or some kind of talk would have come to me. But there was none of any of this. You received a visit, which could not attract attention, otherwise it would have already been noticed. Why did it not attract attention? Because you often receive him. It had to have been a quite harmless visit. A circumstance, however, could make us wonder. From the explanations given by your husband, I was able to deduce that the cigars usually disappeared on Tuesday evening, at the time when he was at the club. What I didn't know, but what you indicated, is that on Tuesday your servant likes to attend the theater."

"I hope you will not draw your conclusions from this circumstance!"

"I don't think so. In fact, it seems to me that the young man appears quite frequently on the premises, but that on Tuesday he lingered a little longer and entertained the housewife."

"That is true, but I can assure that the conversations are quite harmless."

"I never doubted this, especially since the young man—how can I say? —is a little below your level."

"How did you sift that out, Dagobert?"

"It is self-explanatory, madame. Our friend Grumbach has not missed one or two cigars, but six or seven. You remember, according to him, two cigars had been missing from the top layer the day before. In any case, Grumbach took them out himself and thus half involuntarily got the impression presented by the inside of the box. One day later, it seemed to him as if eight or nine pieces were missing. Thus, the disappearance of six or seven pieces. However, one does not smoke six or seven heavy cigars during an hour's chat with the lady of the house, one smokes one. Two at most. Now it looks as if the mistress had encouraged the young man to take a few more cigars when he left."

"That's right, too. But it still does not follow that I, as you prefer to express it, should have entertained myself with someone at a level below my own."

"I beg your pardon, my dearest. For a proper social visit, the housewife might suggest one take along a cigar—one! Of course, without emphasis. To give a handful—or to take them—well, that indicates a certain social distance."

"You are really a pure detective superintendent, Dagobert!"

"At a distance, and yet with a certain sympathy."

"He is a very nice, amiable young man. Did you uncover anything else?"

"Oh, a great deal! I asked myself the question: What kind of young man can come into the house so often, perhaps daily, without any sort of notice? The answer was not difficult. It could only be an official from your husband's office, probably one who has the task of bringing the cashier's key or the daily report to the boss every day."

"Certainly, after business is closed, he brings home the daily report. My husband arranged it this way."

"Which he did very correctly. I know that, too, now, by the way. Because I was recently with your director."

"The things you get up to when you follow a clue!"

"Either one doesn't begin, my dearest, or one begins, but then one must go all the way to the end. Otherwise, it's pointless."

"And what did you accomplish with the director?"

"All I could wish for."

"Let me hear about it, Dagobert!"

"I told him that I had come to patronize a young man—only he was not to betray me to Mr. Grumbach. The director smiled. He knew quite well that if I wanted something from the boss, it would be approved from the outset. Possibly, I admitted, but I would rather not take advantage of our friendship by asking him directly. The director understood, or acted as if he understood, and offered himself at my disposal.

"'What's this about?' he asked.

"'You have a young man in the office,' I replied, 'Now, what's his name? I have such a hideous memory for names! Doesn't matter; it will come. I mean a remarkably tall young man with agreeable manners'— otherwise you wouldn't have liked him, my dearest—'with a beautiful black beard and good teeth. In the evening, he usually delivers papers to Mr. Grumbach's residence.'

"'Oh, that's our secretary, Sommer!' the director interrupted me.

"'Sommer, of course Sommer! How could the name slip my mind! You see, my dear Director, Sommer is indeed a very gifted person, but he's not at the right place in the office doing correspondence. He lacks the final precision and accuracy at work. On the other hand, he would be admirable for dealing with groups. I know that you have been looking for a suitable person for quite some time to head the sales branch in Graz. Wouldn't that be a good spot for Sommer?'

"The director slapped his forehead with his hand.

"'By goodness, that is an idea! There we are, searching until our eyes pop out of our heads and we have the man under our noses! Of course, Sommer is made for it! You haven't exercised patronage on him, rather, your suggestion does us a service. He'll go to Graz. The matter is settled.'

"You see, my dearest, I was lucky enough to be able to play God a little."

"But Dagobert, how could you risk the assertion that the young man is not good for the office?"

"There was no risk in it. I relied on my little bit of psychology. The right office person is always more or less—to a certain extent—a pedant. His job requires him to exercise constant minute precision. Our friend is not a pedant. The right office person doesn't bite the tips of the cigars with his teeth, but cuts them neatly with a penknife or special tool that he carries securely with him if he is a cigar smoker. And there's something else the right office person doesn't do. He doesn't put cigar butts on marble fireplaces. Instead he strives to get to the ashtray and deposits the remains there, always striving to make sure that no trace of ash is left beside it. Our careless young friend, who is imprecise with a cigar stub, probably won't be very precise with office work. He doesn't have it in him!"

"And from this, you immediately concluded that he was the right man for sales?"

"Not only from that, but from the preference you have given him, my dearest. He must be very well-spoken, and he will probably also be a bit of a ladies' man. All this is very admirable when one has to make personal contact with customers."

"One thing you must tell me, Dagobert. You have tried to get rid of the young man because you were worried about my virtue?"

"But, Frau Violet! You know what trust I place in you! But as I knew that the disappearing cigars had passed through your hands, and that you were therefore keeping a secret from your husband, the smoker really had to disappear. It had to be so!"

"A secret, yes. That was the awkwardness for me. I didn't tell my husband immediately. I didn't think of it. And if he had made an issue of it, it would have raised doubts. It would have been embarrassing to me."

"That's just as I understood it, madame. For me, by the way, my carriage must have arrived. If the young man should come to say goodbye, offer him a different variety of cigar for a change, and then this most important matter will be settled."

The End